Unfair LOVE

ANNA KATMORE

To Raff & Bash.

The most unlikely couple

that ever pulled me in their world.

CHAPTER 1

Raffael

Nothing gets me in deeper shit than someone saying, "I dare you."

My excuse? I have none. Thrilling challenges are my weakness. One day, they'll be my downfall for sure. The one tonight only costs me my integrity, thank God. And maybe a little bit more, but that remains to be seen.

My butt is glued to the seat of the horrible brown rust-bucket that almost died of exhaust pipe cancer when I drove it here. All the way through London, pitch-black smoke rose from the 1981 Ford's rear end as if a genie were trying to worm its way out of that porous pipe. Unfortunately, the fog does little to shield me from the judging eyes of the racing community as I roll through the fifty-something pimped cars that turned up to show off and maybe race for some money. Not a bad Friday night.

I kill the engine and get out of the car, leaning against the door. The dubstep beats blaring from all sides of the parking lot behind the closed supermarket in Enfield vibrate through my body. Everything here pulsates, not just the pussies of the two dolly-birds sashaying in my direction. Felix, sitting on the hood of the hot, carbon-gray car that doesn't fit him at all, checks out the twins in their cut-offs and bandeau tops with their knee-high boots. He grins at me. I know what he's thinking. They could save me. But even with the way they look down their noses at me and hold back smiles, I can tell they won't come anywhere near me as long as I'm hanging around this butt-ugly car that I've been forced to drive around with this week. Or for much longer if I can't get one of the many play-bunnies here to kiss me before midnight.

Making out doesn't usually present much of a

difficulty for me. Girls like my Nordic-blond hair that is buzzed short on the sides and left long on top. It keeps falling into my eyes as I level dominant looks on them, my gaze eating them up. But getting close to one of these haughty pigeons with a pile of scrap metal tied to me in a place where the cheapest car still costs more than fifty grand is a challenge. One I might have underestimated. Damn Felix for baiting me so easily with an offer of an airbrush painting for my car. But he's a genius when it comes to that, and what I want will take him days.

What's more, the prospect of fucking Tanja in my playroom was too hot an offer to decline. Tanja, in her black mini, looks a lot better against the shiny Corvette than Felix does. Double wagers with my two best friends—surely, my death.

I've done Tanja on more than one occasion. The slim, ebony-haired beauty loves fetish sex as much as I do, and ever since I eased her into the world of bondage and discipline three years ago, I knew no one else could fulfill my needs as perfectly as she does.

It's almost a shame that I couldn't agree to the

relationship thing with her when the subject came up. She's always wanted the full package. Cuddling and stuff. Not just bondage and punishment. Well, not *only*. Unfortunately, I'm not a cuddly person, and I'm definitely not the right boyfriend for her. Felix would be a lot better in that department. He enjoys keeping her until breakfast after they've slept together, but he's not into kinky sex. Too bad for Tanja. But, all in all, it makes us the perfect little band of friends—with the occasional stranger-fuck once in a while.

"Want me to call some of my friends to kiss you free, Björnsson?" Tanja taunts me with her megawatt smile. Oh, that will bring her an extra spanking, and not a gentle one—at least once I rightfully win her for the coming weekend.

"I don't need your mercy, sweetness," I tell her through a lopsided return-smile. "I'll have none for you either."

She laughs, but I detect that she's thrilled to the bone about what I'm going to do with her. I can see it in her gleaming brown eyes. Felix loosely drapes an arm around her neck, his black leather jacket riding up as he levels me with a sporting glance. "Don't hurt her too bad. She'll cock-block me for days if you go too rough on her."

"*Rough* is what they call me." I waggle my brows. And it's true. In more than one way.

A low-riding white Honda cruises past and glides into the empty parking space behind my current ride, dragging my gaze away from the girl I want to tie up and screw. It's the only free spot left, or the driver likely would have found a space far, far away from the rust-bucket that also sports a tin watering can on the roof. Felix is a sadist. He'd actually do well in a playroom.

The guy who gets out of the Honda wears a shit-eating grin and flips his black ballcap around. The strip between the fabric and the adjustable band captures a few strands of dark hair and makes it flop against his forehead. I've never seen him or his car before at one of these illegal street races, but if he can drive as well as his car is sexy, he definitely came to the right place. If you can handle a sports car, it's easy to make a few grand a night. Most guys here put more effort into pimping their rides than honing their driving skills, though. It's actually shocking how often they overestimate themselves.

I own an apartment in Mayfair, one hundred and eighty square meters on two levels, right beneath the roof of the ninth and top floor. To be fair, half my money came from an inheritance from when my grandmother in Iceland died. She willed me some land that I could sell when I started my architecture studies. But the rest comes from illegal races all over London. I'm good at what I do. In my playroom *and* on the street.

The guy with the hat walks around my hood, not sparing me or the old banger a second glance. I didn't expect it anyway. He aims straight for the Corvette and circles it with a covetous gleam in his eyes, his gaze locked on the car's flawless finish, twenty-one-inch rims, and the license plate that reads: *ROUGH*. Done with his inspection, the man stops in front of Felix, with his hands in his pockets, and narrows his eyes at my best friend. "Are you Raffael?" he asks with a dark south-coast accent.

Oh. Now it's getting interesting. I straighten a little in my lean against the rusty ride and cross my arms over my black and white t-shirt, listening in on what the dude has to say to the Stingray C7's real owner. Tanja casts me a skeptical glance, but I just shake my head.

"Who wants to know?" Felix retorts, keeping his cool.

"My name is Sebastian Rhyse." He holds out a hand, frowning with obvious confusion at Felix's stark red hair. Somebody must have given him a description because I would bet my car—my *real* car—that he expected platinum blond. "I'm new in town and was told the Stingray makes for fine competition."

Felix eases his arm from around Tanja's shoulders and smacks his hand into Sebastian's to shake. "Felix Tyrone. That's not my C7." He sneers at me, then continues speaking to Sebastian. "But it might very well change owner tonight."

I laugh. "You wish."

Sebastian casts me a look over his shoulder. I can see when realization clicks into place at the color of my hair. He tilts his head and lets his gaze roam down the length of my body in a way that holds a surprising amount of interest. His eyes take a while to fix on mine, and then the left corner of his mouth hikes up. "You are Raffael?"

I shrug, a cynical smile riding my lips. "True, I look young for twenty-three years, but I've got my driving license, I promise." I push away from the rust-bucket, unfortunately taking the door handle with me. It clatters to the ground, and I stare at it for a moment with my hands in the pockets of my black skater pants. Yeah, that's just...shit. Sighing, I leave it be and turn to the stranger. "What do you want with my car?"

His sneer makes his eyes gleam. "In the best possible scenario, the ownership papers." Black Maori tattoos emerge from beneath the rolled-up sleeve of his black shirt and run along his entire right forearm. I find the pattern strangely relaxing. Everything is structured within the lines. Rules have always centered me. When I look closer, I see he sports a simple, beautiful leather bracelet on his left wrist that harmonizes well with the New Zealand-style tattoos. That he wears his black watch on his right wrist irritates me a little, though. It's the wrong place for a watch.

"You want to race me?" I demand.

"You've got a reputation. I'm always up for interesting challenges."

Yeah, me, too. I've won several cars in the past, mostly selling them for good money afterwards. On rare occasions, I lost them again in other races, yet I barely ever bet my Corvette. My baby is holy to me. But right now, I only have the scrap metal behind me to offer. And Sebastian doesn't look as if he'll accept the papers to that one. "Sorry to disappoint you. At present, I'm not really in a position to decide on my car."

I'm not even allowed to drive it. And since tonight's race will start in just a few minutes, it's doubtful that a cute bunny will kiss me free before all racers roll toward the starting line. Especially since I haven't even begun to flirt any of them close yet.

Sebastian's straight, dark brows tip toward the bridge of his nose.

"Stupid bet. Long story," I explain without him asking the question out loud.

Felix pulls Tanja between his legs and folds his

arms beneath her breasts. With his chin on her shoulder, he chuckles. "A voluntary kiss from anyone here before the race is over while leaning against"—he nods toward the Ford—"that?"

"Ah, yeah..." Sebastian rubs his neck, looking around the place brimming with beautiful people and even more beautiful rides. He definitely seems familiar with the shallowness of the scene. "That's going to be hard."

Hard, but not impossible. Though I should stop chatting with strangers already and get down to business.

"What are the rules?" he demands, swinging back to Felix. "Girls only?"

What kind of stupid question is that? My friends both grin like lunatics, and Felix waves a relaxed hand. "If Raff thinks he can attract some guys to make out with him, he can do so as much as he likes." He throws his head back and laughs. "Damn, now I wish I'd made this a rule from the start."

The level look in Sebastian's dark eyes raises a weird feeling in my gut as his gaze travels over me once more. He smirks at Felix. "No, you don't." One second later, he closes the distance between us in two determined strides. The next thing I feel is the door of the rusty Ford against my back, and a male body pressed flush to my front. It knocks the wind out of my lungs. Sebastian grabs my face with both hands and lays a fucking kiss on my lips.

Jesus Christ!

My whole body goes rigid. Only my hands clash against the metal of the rust-bucket for help, support, *anything*. But there's no escape from this moment.

The two inches Sebastian has on my six-foot-one frame are unnoticeable as he dips down and tilts his head sideways. When his tongue slips into my mouth and drags across mine in a sensual caress, I can taste his last cigarette on it, mixed with something sweeter, perhaps a Coke. To my utter astonishment, a man's tongue feels very much like a woman's. Only his light stubble scraping against my shaved skin makes the kiss different—and fills it with an unexpected carnality. Hell, this is odd.

And even stranger is that my body wants to give in. Fuck, I'm not enjoying this, am I? Well, no way in hell! My hackles rise at the awareness that the entire racing community of London might be watching this.

The moment is over as fast as it started, and Sebastian lets me go. Lips still in a sensuous curve, he takes a step back and tucks his hands into the pockets of his ripped jeans. He's cool.

I'm not.

With a deep, confused frown, I place my fingertips on my mouth. "Thanks...?" I murmur, not really sure if that's the right thing to say. Then I quickly wipe my palm over my mouth, my gaze darting around the place to check people's reactions. But no one seems to have noticed. Other than my two best friends, that is.

Felix's laughter bounces between the cars as he comes forward and smacks the keys to my Corvette into my open palm. "Here you go, pal. You earned it. That was one hell of a kiss."

"Yeah, get a grip," I snarl, rolling my eyes, fighting to regain the full power of my voice. The raspy sound is so much unlike me...outside my playroom anyway.

Ignoring Sebastian's still-intense gaze, I push

through the guys and head straight for the two sweeties I just won. Tanja smirks at me, watching me come closer. I grab her neck and haul her toward me, pressing my mouth to hers for a hard, deep kiss in an attempt to rid myself of the taste of Sebastian on my tongue.

"See you in my playroom," I purr against her lips, finally centered and back to myself. "Tomorrow at ten."

Letting her go in the next instant, I slide my fingers over the air slits in the Corvette's hood, tracing the smooth finish along the frame of the windshield. "Hey there, beautiful. Miss me?" My heart pounds in anticipation of finally getting back behind the wheel of my baby.

The door opens with the familiar low click, welcoming me in. I glide into the driver's seat, one leg in and one outside the car, my foot still on the concrete. Immediately, the smell of leather surrounds me. No need to slide the key into the slot to start the engine. It works via pushbutton when the key is inside the cabin. The vibration of 490 horsepower shivers beneath me. Caressing the sporty steering wheel like the body of a sexy woman, I close my eyes and revel in the feeling of being back in my personal heaven.

"When you're done fucking your car, come meet me at the scratch line."

I open my eyes to Sebastian's chuckle and give the man, who's draped one arm over my open car door, a curt nod.

Let's race, baby!

The asphalt is still warm from today's scorching temperatures this late June. Best conditions for the tires. They'll stick to the tarmac like a train to its rails.

My heart thumps in sync with the bass from the speakers as I roll in a crawling pace to the starting line. Four cars rev at the scratch, and I take up the space in the middle. The white Honda waits to my left, its driver leveling a daring look at me through the open passenger window. "Bet your car, pretty boy?" he shouts.

The races we stage always require an entry fee of one grand, straight-up. That's standard. Winner takes all. Only in rare instances, the drivers unofficially raise the stakes a little.

An electric feeling rushes through me as I bite my bottom lip. I have no idea what kind of driver he is. Fearful, safe, stupid, reckless? I've never seen him race before. He could be a crack-brained imposter, challenging me even when he's obviously heard of my reputation. Or he could be my match. Losing my Corvette again tonight would so ruin my week. Winning his Honda could make it, though.

My heart beats in my throat. Ah, fuck it. I nod. And Sebastian grins, slowly turning to face front again.

Nikki, a slender doll in black hot-pants and heels so high they could put her level with a skyscraper, walks down the line and takes the entry fee from each driver. I blow her a kiss and wink when I hand her my thousand pounds, a thick wedge of bills that I draw from my pocket. She wishes me luck with a curve of her stark, red-painted lips.

With the money secured with Rob, one of the five line judges, Nikki grabs two checkered flags and takes up position in front of us. Elliot and Master B have been monitoring the police radio. The Japanese genius and the pothead with his shoulder-length dreadlocks are hacking specialists and responsible for giving us the green light. Literally. It's a cakewalk for the programming students to sneak into the traffic system and manipulate a few stoplights to give us free rein down the next two miles of Old-Park Ave and around Bush Hill Park. It's a lap I've done several times already, but not recently. Still, I know every bump in the road, the degree of each curve, and the places where one should ease their foot off the gas if they want to finish the course.

When Nikki raises the flags high above her head, the engines of the white Honda and the dark red Nissan to my right roar like horny lions. I briefly tap the accelerator, too, just to say hello. With her last check to the hacker boys, Nikki's ponytail flies over her shoulder. And then she swings the flags down like the wingbeat of an eagle.

I stomp the accelerator all the way down to the floor and release the clutch. The updated transmission enables abbreviated shifting, and I hack my way through the gears. The Corvette is a sporty little job, easy to handle, and ready for mischief. We fly down the street, passing cars that wait at side roads because of their unscheduled red lights. I don't need to look at them to know their drivers' heads are snapping from left to right in astonishment.

Two-hundred and fifty meters into the race, the Honda, the Nissan, a black BMW, and I are still neck-in-neck. The violet Golf with probably just short of 400 horsepower falls behind. My blood is on fire as we near the first hard curve to the left. This spot will determine who'll take the pole position, as there isn't enough room for four cars to round the corner. We're all good handlers. And we've all got fast cars. But only the most reckless driver will take the lead. And I'm determined to be the one.

I shift down, quickly step on the brakes, and then press the accelerator again, aiming for the shortest possible way around the curve. We're losing the Nissan, and the BMW reacts a nanosecond too slowly, as well. I drift elegantly around the bend, the screeching of the tires promising that I'll soon need a new quartet for the Stingray. The Honda drifts next to me—along the outer curve. It costs him. And here we go... Pole!

Sebastian's Honda snoops at my ass. He's so close, I can't see his headlights or even the hood in my rearview mirror. This is the short side of the park. He'd be crazy to try and overtake me here since I own the track right next to the sidewalk, and he'd lose half a second anyway, being forced to take the outside curve on the long side again.

The Nissan, the BMW, and the Golf are done. Unless Sebastian and I knock ourselves out in this part of the race, the game is completely over for them. No chance at the cash prize.

But the Honda is still a pain in my ass. I can see in the rearview mirror when it gets ready to overtake me, but my accelerator is flat against the floor. Sebastian fights for every inch on the road, and so do I. And when we near the finish line right behind the last curve, our front tires seem like Siamese twins.

One hundred meters left. Enough for the asshole to acquire half a car length of the lead. But I'm still in a better position to drift into the finish. I shift down, tap on the brakes, and feel the Corvette's rear coming along. With no more than two feet of distance between my car door and his, Sebastian does the same and, as if one, we drift around the final curve together, slithering over the finish line with hundreds of celebrating people on both sides.

Fuck! It's not easy to tell who got the crucial final inches to win the race.

With my heart pounding a brutal beat, I pull the Corvette to a halt in the middle of the parking lot and get out. Sebastian has already slammed his car door. While the line judges will need to evaluate the videos and photos on their cell phones to name the winner of the five thousand pounds, Sebastian comes forward, holding his hand up at chest-level. I smack mine into his, giving it a quick press. So much better than kissing the guy. "Awesome race," I compliment him. "Respect."

Sebastian smirks, letting go of my hand. "So it's true what they say. You're one of a kind, Raff."

I don't think I am any longer. He really is my match. Damn, I just hope I didn't lose—

"Tie!" Rob shouts from the huddle of line judges who, until now, had their heads together. "It's a fucking tie!"

"What...?" The word breaks from my hoarse

throat, and I can feel the color drain from my face. Rob and Lauren come running toward us, both holding out spectacular finishing shots on their phone displays, the Corvette and the Honda gliding across the line, completely in sync. If this weren't my car, I would have whistled through my teeth in awe. Right now, I'm as silent as the last sunray of the day.

"Shit, no!" Sebastian lays his hands on his head over his cap, but he takes it with a lot more amusement than I do and laughs incredulously.

I don't care that the prize money will be split in two and I'll more than double my entry fee. I'm going to fucking lose my Corvette tonight! *Again!* Because a tie means—

"We need to trade cars," Sebastian deadpans.

Yes. We have to. It's in the rules. But I don't want to give up my 'vette! What am I going to do with a fucking Honda?

I'm still a little beside myself when Nikki hands each of us our share of the prize money and I slip the wedge of bills into my pocket. A clap on my shoulder makes me snap up my head again. "Now that was impressive for once!" Felix cheers, but his features change, and he cringes the moment he sees my face. "Sorry, dude."

Tanja lays her fingers under my chin and smirks, a daring look in her eyes. "Naw, don't do the sad puppy, Riff-Raff. The Honda is a sexy car, too. You just need to make a little contact, get used to each other." She pulls up her nose like a bunny, taunting me. "She'll love your quirks."

I grab her wrist hard and pull her hand away. The girl obviously wants to get spanked until her ass is the color of a strawberry field. She wouldn't call me Riff-Raff if she didn't want the punishment. Rather roughly, I pull her closer to me and snarl through a smile. "Tomorrow, sweetie. Tomorrow..."

Tanja groans in anticipation. She tugs her hand away when my grip eases and then returns to Felix's side. Lacing her fingers over his shoulder, she rests her chin on them and flashes me a fiery look. She's edible when she does the provocative, wild-cat routine. Too bad I only eat my meals shackled and blindfolded in my *dining room.*

CHAPTER 2

Sebastian

I won the Corvette.

I lost my Honda.

Cheer, or ram my fist into the wall?

Fuck, no clue.

This is my first tie, and I hardly ever lose. Sure, I've wanted this dark beauty from the moment I laid eyes on her twenty minutes ago—and maybe the platinum blond one, too. But *trading* was never my intention.

In the unlikely event that I lose my car in races, I always bring the papers. They're locked in the glove compartment. I've no idea how Raffael will handle this, so I lean against the Honda, my ankles crossed, my arms folded over my chest, and give him a moment to banter with his friends before I cut in. "Are you ready to let go of your ride? Have all the car papers with you?"

He drags his attention away from the girl who seems to be with his red-haired friend—then again maybe not—and nails me with a hard stare. "I haven't been driving my car for a week. Papers are at home. You can follow me."

Nope, he's not happy about the trade, either.

I nod and watch him slip behind the wheel of the Corvette without another word, his forehead creased in frustrated lines. When he pulls the door shut and starts the engine, I get into my own vehicle and push the button to let it purr like a jaguar. The police will likely be here in a few minutes anyway. What the guys did with the traffic lights won't stay undetected for long. The crowd has already started to scatter.

I reverse and line up behind Raffael as he waits with one arm braced on the open window next to his friends. "Key to the Ford is in the lock. Bury it in whatever shithole you dug it out of," he says with a snide grin. It makes me chuckle. Damn, what stupid wagers do these kids come up with when their PlayStations don't work?

Then again, I probably should stop seeing them as *kids*. Raffael said he's twenty-three. That's only two years younger than I am, even though he was right. He hardly looks his age. I almost felt like a pedophile when I kissed him earlier. Yeah, okay, no, I didn't. His eyes have a chilled dominance that more than makes up for the experience his boyish face lacks.

I would say he's absolutely my type. But that would be a lie because I don't actually have a type. I fuck just about anything that promises some good fun—pussy or ass, I don't care. Too bad he doesn't seem to play for both teams. It was evident that I was the first male kiss of his life—it was etched on his face and in his initial tension when I slid my tongue between his lips. Still, not a bad first kiss at all.

When he leaves the parking lot and weaves into the once again flowing traffic, I'm glued to his rear bumper and follow him through London. We pass the bend to my place on Primrose Hill and head straight on to Mayfair. Rich boy, huh? The Corvette said as much, but then it could be his piggybank, too. The moment we turn onto Brook's Mews, and he eases the speed and heads down into the underground car park beneath the tower block, all my doubts are wiped away.

I follow him along the serpentine path to a place that screams "*money*" from all ends. Porsches, Audis, lots of BMWs and even a Lambo in a striking cherry red are all tucked in to sleep here. Raffael aims straight for spot 37 next to a shiny black Jeep that could house a bear family. I park the Honda in 37A, probably the place for his guests.

After turning off the engine, I take a few more seconds just sitting here, my fingers closed tightly around the wheel. A sigh leaves me. I love this car. It's like a loyal pet. A dog that I took in as a rollicking whelp and helped to shape into the finest companion possible. The Corvette is a good trade, though. An upgrade for sure. If it's got character, we'll see.

I retrieve the papers from the glove compartment and finally get out.

Raffael seems to have similar feelings about his

Corvette. He strokes his hand along the roof's edge and down the windshield bar. I swear his lips form the silent words, "*Take care, beautiful.*"

When I sit on the hood of the Honda and wait for him to get his paperwork from his apartment, he looks at me and nods toward the aluminum doors of the elevator on the far side of the space. "We can do all the formalities upstairs. Wanna come up for a beer?"

Sounds better than waiting in the basement. "Sure." I follow him through the garage, marveling at the status symbols surrounding us. The brief *cheep* my car gives when I press the lock button on the key fob is like a last goodbye.

There are two elevators down here, a few meters apart. Raffael calls the one with the *Private* sign, and a red box appears around the square button when the up arrow lights up. Moments later, the doors slide open, and Raffael walks in first. The vertical row of floor numbers is secured with a numeric keypad, and he punches in four digits after pressing the ninth floor. He doesn't make a secret of the code. 2-1-1-2. Perhaps his birthday in December?

The stall is big enough to hold five or six people, marble and mirrors all around. Raffael leans with his back against one side wall, ankles crossed and fingers gripping the handrail at waist level to either side of his hips. I lean against the wall opposite him, my hands deep in my pockets.

Since neither of us speaks a word, it gives me plenty of time to study his face as we ride up to the ninth floor. Penthouse. Man, he's got style. And eyes so Arctic blue, they could freeze the air inside the elevator—even without him doing his best to kill me with a glare. With his platinum hair and the pale skin that he probably can't help, the guy resembles a glacier. A fucking hot one.

"Norway?" I give it a random guess.

The elevator stops, and the doors slide into the walls. "Iceland," he retorts in a cold voice as he exits directly into the living area of his apartment that is illuminated by sporadic spotlights in the ceiling. More come on automatically when he walks farther inside. I push away from the mirrored wall and follow his unspoken invitation, looking around the enormous place.

Graphite-colored slate tiles make up the floor, the white leather couch in the middle of the space between the elevator and the giant windows overlooking Mayfair standing like a crown. The L-shaped sectional faces a low coffee table set on a turquoise angora carpet, and some glass vitrines stand like silent guards in the background. The gaming headset and controller on the coffee table make me grin and search for the entertainment center. Found it. A monstrous flat-screen attached to the wall on the left with a PS4 plus an X-Box One on black shelves beneath it. I knew he was a gamer.

While Raffael turns left into the open dining and kitchen area, I'm still hung up on the winding stairs, obviously leading to the second floor of this apartment. "Damn!"

Raffael chuckles at my impressed cuss, the sound accompanied by the clanging of bottles in the refrigerator door as he pulls it open. I join him, leaning one hip against the giant kitchen island, folding my arms after dropping the Honda's paperwork onto the dark marble surface. He slams the fridge door shut and brings over two bottles.

Hooking the cap of the beer on the edge of the counter, he smacks it open and places it in front of me. Then he unscrews the top of his water bottle and holds it out.

"Don't like to drink before bedtime?" I tease him and grab the beer, clinking it to his anti-drink. "Cheers."

"I don't drink alcohol." He lifts the bottle to his mouth then adds, "At all," before he takes a sip.

In slight wonder, my eyebrows ride a low line as the cold beer trickles down my throat. My unspoken question coaxes his nonchalant shrug. "I like maintaining control."

"Control?" Now the guy whose body seems well-defined though not as muscular as mine has got me seriously curious. "Of what?"

"Of everything." He screws the cap back on his water and puts the bottle down, keeping his slender fingers around it. "People. Cars. But especially...myself. My mind. Alcohol makes you do stupid things."

I raise one taunting eyebrow and speak with the bottle's mouth touching my lips. "Like landing your ass in a bet with a brittle Ford and a kiss?"

"No." He smiles, but it stops short of his eyes. "That was a very controlled bet."

It sounds intriguing. And sad. "You don't let go easily, do you?"

"Never." Raffael laughs. Fuck, even that is a controlled sound, and it makes me want to dig deeper into this guy's psyche. Lots deeper.

He leaves the kitchen and disappears into a room next to the stairs. When he comes back with a pile of papers that must belong to the Corvette, I imagine the room is some kind of office. He throws everything onto the kitchen counter with a blue pen on top. In the racing scene, it's customary that you have a sales agreement for your car ready. Apparently, London runs no differently than Eastbourne, the town where I was born and grew up—and where I've been attending illegal street races since I was eighteen.

I grab the pen and sign both contracts in the specified places. Then I hand over the pen, and Raffael pulls the paperwork towards himself. "It's Friday night," he points out while signing everything next to my name. "You won't find any insurance institution or DMV open before Monday morning to do all the formalities with deregistering the cars and legally changing ownership." He looks up, slowly setting the pen down. "I guess you want to trade tonight regardless?"

Oh yeah, I do. With a grin, I nod. "We can both get a little acquainted with our new rides over the weekend. Damn, I'm dying to find out what your beauty hides under her skirt." He doesn't react to my taunting, only pulls the keyring from his pocket and unfastens the one for the Stingray. With a melancholic sigh, he places it on the pile of car papers. And he gets mine in turn. "I'll come by next week to seal the deal."

Raffael watches the black chip-key for the Corvette disappear into my pocket. "I won't have much time to test the Honda this weekend. A friend's staying over." Only now, his gaze travels up to my eyes. "But you can knock yourself out with mine."

His words ring with the pieces of conversation I overheard him having with Felix's sort-of girl. "The black-haired one?" I probe, taking another sip from the beer. "What is that threesome you and your friend have with her?"

He tilts his head and studies me for a second, his lips curving into a smirk. "Now, wouldn't you like to know?"

"You bet." I put the half-empty bottle down and push my hands into the back pockets of my jeans. "But if you don't want to reveal anything, you could tell me how a guy your age finances this incredible place instead." I spin on the spot, taking everything in once more. It's exceptionally clean. Even the kitchen looks as if it's never been used. "What do you do for a living, dude?"

Raffael laughs—bloody hell, an honest one this time. The sound draws my gaze back to him. "Had a rich grandmother in Iceland," he admits. "And won a few swanky rides I sold."

"Okay, a nice inheritance and some luck at street races. Got it."

He shrugs off my honest impression. "Want a tour of the apartment?"

I must confess that I'm curious how he lives, so I

nod, and he leads the way. Following him into the room that he disappeared into before, I find out that I was right. It's a study, but not only that. There's a huge desk in front of a window to the left, and some barbells along the right side. Above the pressing bench, my attention snags on three tall photographs, perfectly in line with one foot of space between them that, when put together, show the Aurora Borealis over what I assume is Iceland.

"How long have you lived in London?" I demand, strolling toward the windows and looking down at street lights far below. His foreign accent is barely there but, after knowing where he comes from, one can detect it if you're paying attention.

"My family moved to England when I was seven. After my grandmother died, my parents returned to our homeland and live in her house again."

"Without you?"

"I guess I've become a real London kid. Too much space and silence in Iceland. Also, there's the uni here. I hate to quit."

I turn around and find him half-sitting on the edge of the desk, his arms crossed, hawk eyes trained on me. I join him and shove a few papers aside that appear like architectural drawings of a shopping center or something. "Did you do these?"

He unfolds his arms and grips the desk's edge beside his hips, his head dipping to look at the plans. "It's a project for my courses."

"You study architecture?" I lift my gaze and frown. Raffael nods, so my next question comes out a little more incredulous than it was meant to. "Why?"

"Why not?" He mirrors my challenging look.

"I don't know. I guess with all the racing stuff you've got going on, I thought you'd be into something more..."

"Reckless?" He smirks, helping me out with the missing word. When he pushes away from the desk and leaves the room, I follow, closing the door behind me. "Well, I kinda like the structured work as a draftsman," he explains, taking the stairs up. "I find it soothing when things follow the rules, and everything is within defined lines."

I chuckle, loosely running my hand along the curved stainless-steel railing as I follow two steps behind him. "Ah, the control thing."

Raffael casts an intense look and lopsided grin over his shoulder and down to me. "Exactly." Fuck, his light blue eyes play a game with the darkness in a way that makes me tighten my fingers around the handrail.

When he faces front again, I let my gaze roam the huge apartment from an eagle-eye perspective once again. Everything is freaking flawless. There are no dirty dishes in the kitchen, and not a single sock is lying around, which I find highly unusual for a guy his age, living alone. "Who cleans up here? You?"

"Rosa. She comes twice a week, but I try not to make too much of a mess and keep her work easy."

A housemaid. Why am I even surprised?

The landing upstairs splits in two directions with one room at each end and two doors in the middle. The first room he shows me is his bedroom. We stop on the threshold, this obviously being the closest he'll let me get to his sheets. It's just what I expected. A king-size bed made up with dark, satin sheets centered against one wall, and more floor-to-ceiling windows that overlook the city.

"Nice."

There's just enough time to catch a glimpse of a seating bench in front of the windows and a door that probably leads to a walk-in closet beside a low dresser before he shuts the portal to his private space.

The next door leads to a luxurious bathroom done up in stone optic with a walk-in shower behind a completely see-through glass wall and a detached bathtub. I whistle through my teeth. There's a double washbasin made of dark marble, but I have a suspicion that Raffael lives here by himself.

We walk past the second door in the middle of the landing—on purpose, I believe—and he lets me throw a look into the room opposite his bedroom. "The guestroom," he points out.

It's furnished for women. Everything looks much softer and warmer than his own bedroom. The sheets on the queen-size bed are deep red and appear luxurious. There are also several small rose pillows and a makeup table with a tri-fold mirror. Candles are scattered around the place, and on the windowsill sits the only potted plant that I saw in the entire apartment.

"What's her name?" I can't resist asking, leaning

against the doorjamb opposite him and folding my arms over my chest to await his answer.

"Who?"

"The girl you and Felix seem to share. I believe she's the one using this room from time to time, no?"

Raffael pulls his bottom lip between his teeth, scanning my eyes as he obviously deliberates. "Tanja," he admits at last, smiling a little. Apart from him keeping his hands hidden in his pockets most of the time, we lean in an exact symmetrical manner in the doorframe, our toes almost touching in the middle. His wide, tricot-like t-shirt that is parted perfectly into black and white begins to appear like a reflection of his mind to me. He has an utterly beautiful smile but doesn't allow himself to show it because it might be against the rules of his world. It's the Arctic cold versus a strange boyish softness. Both parts are equally hypnotic.

I let the thought pass and stay on track. "So, she's sort of with your friend, but you get to fuck her occasionally, is that the deal?"

Look at that, Raffael has dimples. "I get to *play*

with her a little." His warming gaze switches briefly to the door he didn't yet open. "And they aren't a couple. The three of us have been hanging out and fucking around for like...forever."

Yeah, they actually made that kind of obvious. I laugh and then turn to the secret room. "What's in there?"

"Playground." Even his voice is playful right now. "It's all for experimenting."

"Can I see?"

His upper body tips slightly forward to help him get away from the doorjamb without using his hands. But he pulls one out of the pocket anyway and wraps it around the knob of the mysterious door as he stops, turning my way. "The key to this room is your safeword."

Ah, now it's getting interesting. With a lewd grin, I prowl toward him and halt only inches from his body. I can feel the warmth of him. With a level gaze into his eyes, I lay my hand over his on the knob, close my fingers, and turn to open the door behind him. "I don't do safewords," I drawl, almost too close to his lips.

CHAPTER 3

Raffael

Sebastian's hand is warm. And a little rough. Most likely callused from turning the steering wheel with the heel of his hand, the other always on the gearshift.

I feel his breath on my face, his body intruding on my personal space as if my privacy means nothing to him. Or as if he's doing it on purpose to provoke this gut-twisting feeling. When he turns the knob under my fingers, I move with the opening door to escape him. I'm not usually someone who backs away from confrontation. Tonight, I'm just backing away from too much intimacy.

Sebastian only chuckles at my response and walks into my playroom. I flip the switch next to the door, and a dim, indirect light shines from the gap line along the edge of the ceiling. A mahogany four-poster bed is set against one wall, the mattress draped with deep violet sheets. The shape reflects in the windowpanes along with Sebastian's form slowly wandering around the room.

The cupboards and racks are made of the same dark wood as the bed and line the walls painted a neutral latte macchiato color. I hate glaring hues, especially if they create a skanky atmosphere in a room that is made for aesthetics. Nothing in here is obscene.

I don't need much fancy play furniture either. Or dirty toys. The padded manacles coming down from the cross-piece of the bed really are my favorite. Tanja looks amazing when she hangs from them, blindfolded and quivering for what's to come.

I cross to the bed and lean against one of the posts at the foot of it, observing Sebastian's exploration of the place. The drawers and shelves hold a nice set of floggers and maybe one or two whips. But most of the classy storage room is taken up by ropes of all sorts, chains, cuffs, belts, and bars. I don't need to be brutal to my submissives. Bondage really is my kink. Having absolute control over them. It soothes me like a lullaby does a baby.

When Sebastian wanders past the sound system, he presses the play button, and a hypnotic song drifts from the hidden speakers around the room. He pulls some random drawers open, taking out an item here and there and inspecting it more closely. His fingers glide over the selection of cuffs on the black felt inside one drawer. Then he grabs the sturdy metal eight next to them and turns a curious stare on me, folding it open by squeezing the mechanism to unlock it. "This is how you like to fuck?"

Yes. I much prefer the controlled pleasures in here over going home with a girl where she can get too giddy with excitement in her bedroom. I'm not a big fan of Energizer Bunnies. A nonchalant shrug is all Sebastian gets in answer, though.

His gaze on the metal item in his hand, he opens and closes it several times then weighs it on one palm, tilting his head. "Quite heavy."

It is. And it's only the small edition. Tanja has fragile forearms. Most of the stuff in here is fit especially for her needs. It would probably not close around Sebastian's strong wrists. Mine? Perhaps.

I walk toward him and reach for the metal eight to put it back in the drawer, but Sebastian quickly pulls it away, and I grab air. At the same time, he catches both of my forearms and winds them behind my back faster than I can protest. "What the—?"

A click follows, and I feel the heavy metal encircling my wrists, keeping them in a tight lock. Startled and pissed, I try to look over my shoulder, but I almost bump noses with Sebastian. His face is so close that I hold my breath with shock.

His fingers are still around my wrists, holding them in place, even though I obviously can't move them. His warmth seeps into my skin. "What's your safeword?" he rasps with a deep look into my eyes.

Shit! I laugh. "That's none of your business. Now, let me free."

"Mmm, I don't think so." He reaches around me to grab a black band from another drawer he'd left open. A dangerous sneer on his lips, he unfolds it and holds it up in both hands, a dirty promise in his chestnut eyes. In utter confusion, I frown at him, taking two steps back until the wall stops me. He's in front of me before I can escape and lays the blindfold over my eyes, tying it at the back of my head.

I stiffen. Fucking hell, everything is dark. My breathing hitches to match my accelerated heartbeat.

"This room is for experimenting?" Sebastian's hot breath dampens the skin behind my ear with his whisper. He's setting off the weirdest kind of goosebumps all down my neck. "So, let's experiment."

My lips part, and I pant. Jesus Christ! I need to get out of here.

But I can't see a thing, and the stupid cuffs at my back only open with the right push of the mechanism—which I can, no way in hell, reach. This toy isn't made for playing alone.

Gentle fingers grab my chin, turning my head exactly where Sebastian wants me. His voice is so calm and low, it creates a multitude of edgy shivers running along my body. "Your safeword, Raff?"

I haven't spoken the word out loud in years. I'm

never, *ever* at that end of the deal. "Come on, you're not playing this kind of game," I try to reason. "Take off these fucking cuffs and, for Christ's sake, the blindfold."

"Why?" He slips his hands under my shirt, running his fingers slowly upward over my taught abs. I jerk, but there's no chance of getting away from here. His hands glide to my back and down over the curve of my ass. "Don't like being..." He squeezes. Good God! "At my mercy?"

I'm getting much too warm, which again spikes a panic inside me. My neck bristles. Burning waves of adrenaline shoot through my veins. Everything centers in my lower gut. Holy fuck!

"Safeword..." Sebastian drawls against my lips. "Now."

The unfamiliar scent of sun-warmed skin beneath a light layer of musky shower gel invades my nose. I squeeze my eyes tighter beneath the blindfold and tilt back my head. The asshole starts kissing my neck. And though I hate him for it, I can't regret the sensation.

What the fuck is wrong with me?

As he paints slow circles on my skin with his tongue, I hoarsely groan one single word. "Titanium."

"Good..." Sebastian's chuckle against my throat is dangerous, confusing as hell, and all I can concentrate on. "I'll try and keep that in mind."

When his hands move back to the naked skin on my stomach and chest, a tremble overtakes my body. "Seriously, I'm grateful that you kissed me free from that heap of scrap metal at the race," I croak. "But I'm not into guys."

"Are you sure?" He shoves up my tee and sinks to his knees to kiss a trail along the valley between my abs, giving my belly button a flick with the tip of his tongue. "Because there's a bulge in your pants that says differently."

I know that. Shit, this can't be happening!

"It's not what it seems." *I swear.*

Sebastian's fingertips brush my skin right above the waistband, and my muscles twitch. Trapped against the wall, I sense when he stands up again. "Is it not?" His dark voice comes much too close to my ear, and his stubble rubs against my cheek. "Or is it perhaps exactly what I think, and you're already imagining what my tongue feels like on your cock?"

My nostrils flare with my too-fast breathing. This is getting out of control. I *can't* have things out of control. Ever.

Sebastian grabs my belt, and my hips jerk at his rough pull as he unbuckles me.

My heart bangs so violently against my ribcage, I fear it might knock me out. I lean my head back against the wall. There's only one word on my mind now. "Ti—"

Sebastian crushes his mouth to mine, cutting off every sound. He presses his tongue between my lips and hard against my own as if he wants to push the word right back down my throat. And all I can do is let him.

His fingers let go of my belt and hook beneath the blindfold instead. As he pulls it off my head, his face is still so close that I can feel his breath. He growls through a tiny, amused smirk. "You little fuckin' coward."

Only inches separate our eyes. Our gazes lock with an intensity that burns into every cell of my body. The moment between us seems endless as the air around us ignites with fire. I can barely breathe. Then he leans in the last inch and molds his mouth to my lips once more. His tongue has lost the last bit of cigarette smoke and gives way to the taste of corona. It drags against mine, sensual and slow, causing my eyes to almost shut. His body presses harder against my front as he reaches around to my back and slides his fingers through mine, squeezing briefly. My fingers close, too.

In the next instant, Sebastian unlocks the cuffs. The weighty metal slips free of my wrists and into my hands. It's something to hold on to when he eases away from the kiss. My eyes snap open again.

Warmth surrounds the darkness in his eyes. As he takes two slow steps back, there's just the slightest twitch of the left side of his mouth. "Thanks for the car, Raff..."

Then he walks out of the room and, by God, I can't follow him. Sagging against the wall behind me, I need a minute to catch my breath.

Or maybe five.

I rub my hands over my face, then shove them

through my hair, resting them on the back of my neck. My gaze nailed to the ceiling, I feel every inhale and exhale scorching through my chest. What. The. *Fuck!?*

Struggling to get a grip again, I close my eyes and run my tongue over my lips. I can still taste Sebastian inside my mouth. He shouldn't have—

And *I* shouldn't have...

This is so wrong.

Blowing out an extended breath, I open my eyes again and focus on the door that he disappeared through. When I finally manage to make my shaky legs carry me downstairs, the place is quiet and empty. Sebastian has left. And he took the papers to the Corvette with him.

*

Counting sheep is pointless. Really. In the end, I only managed to keep my mind from wandering back into the playroom for a time while lying on the satin sheets in complete darkness. And how far did I get? 3567. When the sheep started to turn into white

Hondas, I tossed the covers aside and trudged downstairs to grab a glass of water. Then I started the X-Box. *Grand Theft Auto* is a better solution to bringing one through a night than counting fucking sheep jumping over imaginary fences.

I got a couple of hours of sleep on the couch near morning. And dreamed of cigarette kisses. Man. My body was drenched in sweat when I woke up.

For nearly forty minutes now, I've been standing under the shower behind the glass wall, trying to wash away the awkward feeling of having broken the rules. Well, one rule. *The* rule. Jeez. I press more shower gel into my hand and lather up my body from neck to toe—for the fifth time since I turned on the water. But the feeling of wanting to arrange things in tidy lines won't go away.

Eventually, I turn off the spray and towel myself dry. Then I brush my teeth—for like seven minutes or something, but that helps as little as it did last night. I can still feel Sebastian's sensual touch on my tongue. Squeezing my eyes shut, I add another minute of cleaning, then I rinse my mouth and rub my face dry with a fresh, soft towel. It feels comfortable against my skin. Perhaps if I press it over my mouth and nose long enough, I'll fall into a coma and can reboot my brain. Clear out all these strangely sweet memories of yesterday.

My cell phone ringing in the kitchen stops me from knocking myself out. I hang the towel back on the rack bar and trot downstairs, barefoot, wearing only baggy, black pants and a fresh gray t-shirt.

Tanja's name flashes on the display.

"Morning, sweetie. What's up?" I greet her.

"Sad news. I can't stay overnight this weekend." Regret rings in her voice. "My auntie Clarissa invited the whole family for brunch tomorrow. Mom will kill me if I don't go."

Squeezing my eyes shut, I let out a deep growl.

"You want a raincheck for a full weekend next month, or split the days?" she gives me the choice.

I need to fuck. A girl. Soon. "No cancelling. Today is fine."

"Okay, I'll be there in an hour." She hangs up, and I toss my cell phone back onto the counter. Then I open the fridge, needing to sort something. Anything. Five beer bottles are lined up in the inside pocket of the door. Last night, there were six. I turn them so their labels are all perfectly in line. They're for visitors—primarily for Felix when he comes over. Sprite and water, the two main things that keep me hydrated through my life, fill up the top shelf in the fridge, and beneath those, there's a box with some leftover Mexican food from my last lunch. I open the lid and smell. Still good enough for a lonely dinner tonight after Tanja leaves.

Closing the lid, I put it back, centering it on the glass shelf since there's nothing there to arrange it with. Then I divide the apples in the bottom shelf into two groups. Sweet ones on the left, and sour ones on the right. There's one that is neither red nor green, really. A fucking mix that doesn't fit into either side. I take it out and eat it, slamming the door shut.

Ten minutes later, I tidy up my desk, reordering the papers that Sebastian shoved aside last night, and then I press some weights on the bench. I'm not a fan of people blowing their body up to balloon versions of themselves, but I like to keep in shape, and keep my muscles decently defined.

Sebastian is a little burlier than I am. I assume he started working out quite early in his youth so his body shaped up into its current dominating form. It looks natural on him.

Jesus Christ, when did I even notice those things?

Clenching my teeth, I press the bar faster and more aggressively until my biceps burn, and sweat beads on my forehead.

The doorbell rings. I hook the bar onto the rack, wipe my face with the hem of my t-shirt, and pad through the apartment. I don't need to ask or look through the peephole to know who's outside. It's ten o'clock. Tanja is always on time. And she never takes the private elevator to my flat.

I open the door and grab her arm, pulling her in without a word of greeting. Her brown doe eyes grow even bigger as she stumbles into my apartment. "Nice to see you, too," she mutters, but immediately presses her lips together at my silencing scowl. I let her step out of her sandals that match her short, white summer dress, then grasp her wrist and haul her upstairs, right into the playroom. Still in the doorway, I rip my belt from my pants, wind both her hands behind her back, and tie them together roughly. It coaxes out a little groan of surprise from her. I don't give a shit. Instead, I push her forward so she falls onto the violet bed sheets. Then I slam the door shut, yank off my t-shirt, and fling it at her chest.

*

Saturday evening, I lie on the couch, one arm folded behind my head, the other hand resting on my stomach. Tanja left two hours ago. She safe-worded me some time in the afternoon because she demanded that she be able to still sit tomorrow at the family brunch.

Calm for the first time in twenty-four hours and breathing evenly, I enjoy the feeling of being spent. Of having everything under control again. Of still knowing who I am. Except there's a small pile of papers on the coffee table that's been mocking me since I dropped my limp body on the couch earlier.

The key to Sebastian's Honda lies on top. My gaze is glued to them, my bent knee tipping left and right in a lulling rhythm. Lips pressed together, I force myself to look out the window instead of at the table. But the things keep taunting me out of the corner of my eye. Growling, I glare at them again. Ah, fuck it. I push myself up from the couch, grab the key from the table, slip into my sneakers, and head down to the underground car park.

As soon as I exit the elevator, my gaze snags on the empty parking spot, 37, the usual sleeping place of my baby. My heart pings. Breathing deeply, I walk to the white racing car in 37A and unlock it by pushing the button on the key fob. When I open the door, a wave of Sebastian's very personal scent of musk and sun rays with the faintest hint of cigarette smoke hits me square in the face. I regret leaving my cozy place on the couch for this. It's fucking torture, rubbing salt into the wound of losing my Corvette.

Still, I ease into the driver seat and place both hands on the wheel. Sebastian might be a little brawnier than I am, but we're almost the same height. The body-contoured seat is in a perfect position for me. After running my hands slowly around the wheel in a salutatory caress, my gaze wanders across the dashboard and through the interior of the car. Dark gray leather and chrome. Looks quite nice.

"All right… Let's see what you're made of, little one," I murmur, slamming the door shut and starting the engine. The Honda gives a nice purr, but what catches my attention first is that there's no real speedometer in the dashboard behind the wheel. Goddammit! Everything lights up blue and white, transmitting the feeling of driving a virtual car. Who fancies that shit? I want a real needle to move when I step on the gas.

Already frustrated, I slip on the parachute-like belt harness that is similar to the one in the Corvette—thank God—closing it in front of my stomach with a smooth click. The rearview and side mirrors need only minimal adjustments before I back out of the parking spot and let the baby snoop some London air.

I take the street out of town to really test the Honda's talents. There's not much traffic keeping me down, so soon enough, I can floor the little racer and head down the M25. It's easy work, moving through the five gears, but the misfiring when running at low annoys me almost as much as the smell in here. Sebastian must have updated the engine control unit with some special software to change the fuel injection. Flames shooting from the exhaust pipe is so last decade. I snort. Showoff.

Rolling down both windows completely, I welcome the racing night wind inside, clearing my head of the permanent reminder of how Sebastian's smell edged into my mind last night when we—

Fuck, no. Instead of going there, I turn up the music that's been so low since I stepped in that I barely even noticed it. *Euphoria* from Loreen plays. A tiny flash drive sticks out from the port beneath the computer board, apparently filled with Sebastian's personal playlist. A cynical grin sneaks to my face. Well, he can enjoy some dubstep until we meet again to settle the trade.

I fly down the almost empty motorway, taking the exit twenty minutes later to test how the car handles the road on curvier, country terrain. And this is where I quit.

Although the low-slung car cuts a fine figure on

the asphalt, the tires lack a couple of inches in width to guarantee the same driving comfort I'm used to from my baby. She sticks perfectly to the street, not jerking a millimeter, even in hard curves. Unless I want her to. As for Sebastian's car, this one is a drifting machine. Already around the second bend, I struggle to keep it nailed to the road instead of sliding out onto the bank.

Not for me. No thanks.

On the next straightaway, I stomp into a full braking maneuver that presses my body into the belt harness, and pull off a 180-degree turn in the middle of the empty street. Then I race it home in the best time this little sweetie can manage. Mine would have beat it by at least three minutes. Duh.

Back in my apartment, I head straight to my study and boot up the computer. Settling the deal next week? My ass. I'm not keeping this uncontrolled white piece of work. No fucking way.

I open the browser and type *Sebastian Rhyse, London* into the search field. Let's see what Google comes up with.

It throws out a lot of pictures that are obviously

not him and then displays some info about guys with a missing *E* in the last name. Okay, that's a dead end. So, what else? Eyes narrowed to slits, I log into my Facebook account, which I barely ever use. I'm more an Instagram type of person, but the battery of my phone died while I was out, and I didn't take the time to plug it in yet.

There are a million Sebastian Rhyses on Facebook, but most of them are based in the United States. Only three live in England, and only one of them has a white Honda as a profile picture. "Bingo." I let the *B* pop on my lips.

Sebastian has set his account to private. Mostly. But in the info section, it says he used to live in Eastbourne, even went to college there, then was employed for several years at a software company in the South afterward. For the last couple of months, he's worked as a coach in a local fitness center not far from here. Also, his birthday is January 7th.

Clicking the link to the website of the fitness center, I find a list of trainers and even their working schedules and company emails. For a minute, I consider writing to him, asking him to take his shitty car back and demand the keys to the Corvette. But, apparently, he works tomorrow from ten to five. My usual cold grin curves my lips. I think I'll pay him a visit instead.

I write down the name and address of the fitness center on a piece of paper, shut down the computer, and head upstairs to bed. It's almost one in the morning. Time to catch up on some sleep.

CHAPTER 4

Sebastian

"Forty-seven. Forty-eight. Come on, two more! Forty-nine. Aaand..." With the bright sunshine from the tall windows behind me in her face, Christina struggles up one more time. Sweat coats her face, her arms, her ample breasts. Just...everywhere. "Perfect!" I give her an encouraging cheer, still holding her ankles after she finished her set of crunches. The black hot-pants and tank she wears sport sweaty patches in places that automatically draw the attention.

I make an effort not to ogle those spots because I take my job at Podium Fitness quite seriously, and checking out the girls as they train is absolutely unprofessional. When they come by for a chat at the reception desk after their workout, freshly showered and changed…that's a whole different matter.

"Ten minutes easy run on the treadmill," I instruct Christina as I stretch from my squat and extend a hand to pull her from the mint green mat in the middle of the huge training room. "Then five minutes walking to cool down and some stretching before you hit the shower, girl."

With a broad smile, the twenty-year-old student refastens her blond ponytail and jogs off toward the back of the gym where a selection of high-tech training equipment stands. Only a handful of them are in use now, it's early hours, still.

I like Sunday mornings in the fitness center. They're so much quieter than afternoons and evenings during the week. Gives me a lot more time to dedicate to each person asking for advice and support while they work out.

With Christina's ankle sweat still on my palms, I swipe my hands on my dark gray shorts and return to reception, where a pile of membership cards waits to be signed and finished before their owners can pick them up at their next visit. I grab the armrest of the swivel chair that I shoved to the back earlier when Christina called me for aid, and pull it toward the desk. Just about to lower myself, I freeze, staring into the face of a platinum blond Icelander.

Raffael sits across from me on the brown leather couch in the brightly lit lounge, the long sleeves of his white hoodie shoved up to his upper arms, his fingers laced over his stomach. His long legs, clad in light blue jeans, are placed in a wide straddle. Even though his eyes are shielded by turquoise, mirrored sunglasses, his cold look hits me and causes pinpricks.

Slowly, my fingers slide away from the armrest of the chair, and I straighten again. "Well, hi there." This is quite a surprise—not seeing him again sooner than expected, but that he actually figured out just *where* to find me. People who make an effort always impress me. I grab my black watch and fasten it around my right wrist, mumbling, "I thought we were supposed to meet sometime next week?" Then I put the leather bracelet I got on a vacation to New

Zealand on my left arm.

"I want my car back." His tone is just as flat as his expression. Outside of that, he doesn't move one muscle. Fuck, but he's hot when he pulls off the iceberg.

"And I'd love to catch my little niece a unicorn for her third birthday." With a cynical grin, I tilt my head. "Not happening."

After a quick lick, Raffael drags his bottom lip between his teeth. "What do you want with the Stingray? It's not even your style."

Sure, I've been missing the Honda an awful lot since I stroked it goodbye in the underground car park in Mayfair, but the Corvette is magnificent. Extravagant comfort, wicked grip on the street, and undoubtedly worth a handful more than my former ride. "I dig the smell in it," I tease him, my smile growing a little warmer now. "Hot lady on the outside, and all Icelandic snowscape within." I grab a tiny pack of jelly beans with the gym's logo from the basket on the counter and toss it across the lounge at Raffael. "But here's a little consolation for you."

He catches the purple sachet with one hand, his

face still etched in titanium. Then he slowly rises from the couch and walks over. "Let me win it back."

"And risk losing both?" I grimace with a sneer. "Mm, not today." I pick up the yellow pen from the stack of unsigned cards and let it run through my fingers. "But you really should give new things a chance from time to time, Raff. The pleasures might surprise you." And with a face and body like his, there's currently no other guy in the world that I'd rather fuck. He's hot temptation.

Stopping on the other side of the counter, the jelly beans gripped tightly in his fist, he stares at me through his mirrored shades, clearly deliberating his next words as thoroughly as I did my innuendo. "I'm just not a Honda type of person."

Yeah, that's what he tried to make me believe Friday night in his playroom, too. And then he sported a boner.

"What's wrong with it?"

He folds his arms on the counter. "Your car shoots flames."

Dropping the pen, I brace my palms on the desktop and lean forward, fixing him with a stare through the turquoise shield only inches away from my face. "Because it's got fire in the ass," I drawl.

Raff lets a cool, provocative smile slip. "Yeah, I don't fancy burning farts so much, you know."

Does he actually know how sexy he looks when he smiles, even when he says shit like that to fend off what he hasn't tasted? I doubt it.

The phone on the desk starts to ring, but I'm not yet ready to pull myself out of the light scent of falling snow that his skin seems to emit every minute of the day. For two rings, we're both just frozen in the moment. Until he nods his chin to the side. "The phone's ringing. Aren't you going to answer?"

"And your cock is itching for the unknown. What are *you* going to do about it?"

A moment passes. Then, somewhat resigned, Raffael presses his lips into a pale line and sighs deeply. "You don't know me at all, Sebastian."

Since his voice has lost the banter, I turn serious, too. "Then give me a chance to change that."

Slowly, he shakes his head. Too bad. The phone stops ringing. I sigh, straightening from the reception desk. "Anyway, after seeing how you live, I believe you've got enough money to buy a new Corvette, don't you?"

Facing me down, he unfolds his arms and starts fingering the jelly bean sachet on the counter. "I have enough money to buy a Corvette *and* a new Honda...after I send yours to the scrap press." It's quite a surprise when he pulls the sunglasses from his nose and looks me in the eyes. "But I'm sure you wouldn't want that."

Bricking my baby? My eyebrows bulldoze down as I feel a hurtful sting in my chest. Now it's my turn to shake my head.

"I know that *you* know what it's like to brighten up a car over months until you're totally in love with it," he reasons, his voice still low and edged with barely detectable emotion. But it's there. And I understand what he means.

Still, just pulling out of a deal isn't my style. So, I expel a deep breath and purse my lips, pondering for a moment. There's something I've really, really wanted since last Friday in his apartment. Maybe we can make another deal to undo the first one. "I'll trade back under one condition," I say without so much as blinking.

"What do you want?" There's hope edging his voice, even though he knows better than to let it come up so quickly—and without hearing the conditions.

"Two hours in your playroom," I demand.

Raff pinches the spot between his eyes. "Seb—"

"With your friend, Tanja."

His shocked gaze zaps up to my face again.

"I found the toys that you play with quite intriguing. Unlike you, I enjoy testing new things." I give a nonchalant shrug. "And since you guys obviously hand the girl back and forth already, I assume she's open for others, too."

"I...that's not my decision to make." Lines of confusion and discomfort crease his forehead. "She doesn't even know you."

"She doesn't have to be afraid. You'll be there the entire time to take care of her."

That flusters him even more, if the way his eyes narrow is any indication. "Tanja normally chooses her partners herself."

"Well, then..." I grab one of the gym's white

business cards from the stack on the counter, flip it around, and scribble my telephone number on the back. "I guess you've got some persuading to do." With a grin, I slide the card across the counter. "Call me when you've got her agreement."

Raffael stares at me as if I just killed Santa. A muscle ticks in his jaw. I swear the guy can drop the temperature in a room with only a look.

And I don't give a fuck.

He smacks his hand on the card and pulls it off the counter, tucking it into the back pocket of his washed-out jeans. No goodbye. Just the door swinging behind his sexy backside as he leaves.

For a moment, I look after him. Then I turn back and begin to smile, meeting Christina's eyes as she emerges from around the corner. "You done for today?"

*

The light from the TV illuminates my dark living room in a series of flashes. I lounge on the couch, feet stacked on the coffee table, watching some crime thriller while I munch on a turkey sandwich with bacon, veggies, and mayo.

A quiet little pop from my cell phone snags my attention, and I put the snack back on the plate, licking my fingers. I wipe them on my jeans before I unlock the display with my fingerprint and open the WhatsApp message from an unknown number.

Tomorrow evening. 6 o'clock.

A surprised smile creeps to my face. Now that was fast. I save the contact as *Iceland*, then toss the phone aside and finish my sandwich.

CHAPTER 5

Raffael

The two checks beside my message to Sebastian turn blue. Since there's no return text, he probably agrees. When the display fades to black, I drop the phone next to my thigh, but I have a really bad feeling about this. On the other end of the couch in my living room, Felix looks at me, seemingly quite uncomfortable, too. "Don't leave her alone for one minute with this guy. Understand?"

Of course. I nod. "She'll be safe with me." If Sebastian makes even one wrong move, I'll break every fucking bone in his body.

The only one who seems just fine with the harebrained idea is Tanja. Sitting on Felix's lap, she smirks and enjoys his fingers stroking up and down her back under her dark gray sweatshirt. "You two worry too much," she chides us. "Since when are you both so scared if I'm having fetish fun with some other guy? It's not the first time, you know. And Sebastian doesn't seem like a monster to me."

Because she didn't see him in the playroom when he was here last. I snort. The full story of that night will be forever my secret, though.

"He doesn't know the rules of that world," I growl and press my lips together so vigorously, I'm sure the area around my mouth looks as if I've sucked on a lemon.

"I'm sure he'll behave...just right." Tanja comes crawling across the couch and cuddles against my side. I put my arm around her shoulders—for her comfort, not mine. She rests her head against my chest, and I know precisely where her gaze wanders. To the very abstract painting on the wall across from the couch, the one that was drawn and autographed by the three of us.

I'm not a good painter, that's Tanja's great talent.

But she brought a huge, white canvas and a backpack full of oil and acrylic colors to my apartment two years ago and forced Felix and me to do some artistic shit with her on that thing. If I'd had a choice back then, I'd have gotten my pencil and ruler and would have drawn the perfect house for her barely recognizable elves and fairies. But the sadist just said, "Let the colors spread."

Color shouldn't just *spread*, goddammit. It should be put precisely within the lines of geometrical forms and bodies. But not with Tanja. She always tells us that her paintings need to be as free as she is. Even after all this time, I'm still trying to find the order within the chaos of colorful blots and smudges. The rainbow Felix painted across the upper right side helps a little with that and keeps me from getting a cramp in my brain whenever I look at it. But once we were done and put our names in a triangle at the bottom, it was clear that I would have this work of art and mark of friendship forever on my wall.

"You know, when you look at your part from the door, it resembles some sort of pumpkin," Tanja muses. "But from here, it always reminds me of a beautiful rose blossoming."

"Because it's red," I deadpan.

"No. Because it's got the dark spots in all the right places."

I wind a strand of her ebony hair around my finger and gently tug twice as I tease her, "It was meant to be a car riding over all your pixies."

Laughing, Tanja sits up and smacks me on the upper arm. "You're so crackbrained, Raffael Björnsson!"

I love it when she tries to get the pronunciation of my last name right—and fails. *"Ég elska þig líka,"* I retort with a smirk, telling her in my native tongue how much I love her. Then I push her off me and rise from the couch.

Stacking the plates that we ate our pizza on, I carry them into the kitchen and put them into the dishwasher. Felix brings the three glasses and adds them to the load. "Does he really want you in the room when he has his way with her?" he asks in a low voice, his face scrunching with concern. "That's just weird, isn't it? Expecting you to watch them fuck."

"Totally," I murmur, mirroring his expression. Then again, I didn't tell my best friends that Sebastian is obviously bi and will perhaps get an additional kick out of me being there...like a voyeur. Either way, I don't trust the guy, and it's good that Tanja won't be alone with him in a room full of cuffs and whips.

I follow Felix to the foyer where Tanja finishes buckling her sandals, and lean against the wall while both slip into their jackets. Tanja comes over and kisses me goodnight on the cheek. Felix just knocks his hand into mine then opens the door for Tanja. I hear him ask her on the way out, "Wanna come to my place tonight?"

Her happy, "Hm, okay," promises some fun later for both of them, and it makes me chuckle. The most fun I will have for the rest of the night is probably painting pictures in my head of the scenarios that will happen tomorrow in my playroom. Jeez. A cold shudder runs through me.

*

On Monday evening, I check my wristwatch for the hundredth time. It's ten after six. Tanja said she couldn't come earlier, but when she's not on time, it surprises me. I send her a message asking where she is. Her reply confuses me even more.

We'll be a little late. Don't worry. I'll explain everything later.

With eyes narrowed to slits, I drop onto the couch and send her another message demanding: *Who is we?*

Sebastian and I.

Oh, really? Now isn't that great? Grinding my teeth, I fling the phone aside and start my PS4 for some *Fortnite.* I'm certainly not going to pace a canyon in the floor while waiting for the lovebirds to come and fuck in my apartment.

Shooting zombies helps me vent my frustration. A little. Leo, Thomas, Carol, and George, the people on my team, are great at making me smile. I have no idea what they all look like because I only ever hear their voices through the gaming headset, but they're funny people, and almost feel like a second family as soon as I get online. Well, third family, I guess, right after my own blood, and then Tanja and Felix.

I completely lose track of time, so when the doorbell suddenly rings at a quarter past eight, I startle. After a quick goodbye to my virtual friends, I stop the PS4 and then go to answer the door. Sebastian's and Tanja's relaxed laughter drifts inside even before I open. The acrid taste climbing up my throat is most uncomfortable. But to think it couldn't get worse was a mistake.

When I finally catch sight of them, Sebastian has his arm loosely draped around Tanja's neck as she clutches her handbag to her chest and grins up at his face. I greet them with an arched eyebrow, gripping the door hard as I hold it open.

"Hello, pretty boy," Sebastian drawls with a smirk and pats my cheek, walking in with Tanja still at his side.

I knock his hand away with unmistakable force and growl at Tanja, "Where have you been?"

"Just in—" The rest of her words get muffled by Sebastian's hand pressing to her mouth, and she giggles against it. My brows dip into a deep frown as I slam the door shut.

Sebastian leans so close to her face that his nose brushes her cheek, but his gleaming chestnut eyes nail me alone. "Do you think the snowflake is jealous?" he purrs against her skin.

Does *he* think this is funny? "Yeah, go fuck yourself."

Tanja should know how much I dislike when people aren't punctual. Just her luck that it's not my turn to discipline her upstairs tonight, or she would walk home later with her ass as red as a *Stop* sign and bite marks all over her body.

Sebastian hangs up his leather jacket on a hook and helps Tanja out of her long, black trench coat. She obviously only wears that today to hide the sexy schoolgirl outfit underneath—a blue plaid skirt the length of a ruler and a simple black bandeau-bra to cover her breasts. As she leans down to unzip the inside of her black over-knee boots, he stops her, with a sound swat to her behind.

Tanja takes a squeaking leap into my arms and then twists around to face his grin. This time, he only looks at *her* when he asks, "Mind leaving them on for a little while longer? I like to unwrap my presents myself."

Jeez. I roll my eyes and then straighten my white button-down shirt that Tanja creased when she jumped at me. "Shall we...?" I grumble, waving my arm toward the stairs in a cynical gesture.

Sebastian takes Tanja's hand and pulls her to him, then slings his arms around her, lifts her briefly, and turns back around to me with her in a tight embrace. Taunting me from behind her shoulder, he drawls, "Impatient to watch us play?"

"Just want to get this over and done with." I knock my shoulder so hard against his when I pass them that he automatically lets go of Tanja. "And get my car back," I growl, leading the way upstairs. After I shove the door to the playroom open, I let Sebastian walk in first, and snatch Tanja's hand to keep her with me for a second.

My deep frown is enough to make her whisper, "He caught me in front of your house and invited me to coffee. He wanted us to get comfortable with each other before coming here and make sure I really wanted this." She squeezes my hand with an encouraging and soft expression. "See? I told you he isn't a monster." Then she follows Sebastian into the room where he already sits in the wide, black leather chair by the window, his hands folded behind his head, waiting for us.

His dark blue t-shirt slips up just enough to reveal a strip of suntanned skin above his low-rise blue jeans. The way his long legs are planted on a wide straddle would draw everyone's gaze to his crotch, not just mine. But it makes me feel uncomfortable anyway, so I take the opportunity to turn around and close the door quietly instead of just slamming it shut like I want.

Tanja takes a shy seat on the bed, and I come to lean against the post next to her, folding my arms. I guess we're both a little uncertain as to what he's going to do. But instead of beginning with anything, he continues lounging in the chair and just smirks at us. "You two make a cute couple, do you know that?"

Tanja throws a quick glance at me that I catch out of the corner of my eye, but I only lift a brow at Sebastian.

He lowers his hands to lace them over his stomach

and then scoots a little deeper into the chair. Something about this must amuse him because he hasn't lost his shit-eating grin since he stepped foot in my apartment.

"Now..." he begins slowly, taking his time to inhale and exhale before he goes on. "After your sweet girlfriend explained in quite some detail—hot detail I might add—what you usually do in this room, I'm sorry to disappoint you." His warm and almost apologetic gaze slides to Tanja. "I'm not into physical pain, and you'll never find me hurting a woman." He grips the armrests and pushes himself up to his feet. Slowly. "I understand that this room comes with certain rules." With a prowl, he crosses straight in front of me and levels me with an intense look, standing just a foot away. His voice drops a notch but then gets all the more haunting. "Rules that we're going to abandon tonight."

I unfold my arms as my lips start to form the word, "*What*", but no sound comes out. Tanja grabs my hand and squeezes briefly with her warm fingers. Her head tilts up to me, and it's clear she obviously wants me to listen to Sebastian before throwing him out.

Fine. I shut my mouth again. Understanding our silent conversation, Sebastian nods, seemingly satisfied. As he turns away and strolls toward the chest of drawers with the many bondage toys inside, he continues in an alarmingly calm tone. "We're all here voluntarily, because Raffael wants his Corvette back. You know that you can stop or leave whenever you want. No one has to do anything that he or she doesn't like."

On the way, he pushes play on the hi-fi system, and the trance-like music that Tanja and I used yesterday continues. He gives a small incline of his head, apparently appreciating the sound. Next, he opens the second drawer of the mahogany chest and comes back with a simple black satin band. It's too slim to use for blindfolding, but for tying somebody's wrists, it's perfect. That his daring gaze is on me and not Tanja speeds up my heartbeat, unease skittering through me.

He circles me so close that his chest brushes my arm, and I once again catch a whiff of sun rays in South England. Standing immobile, I let only my eyes follow him until he's behind me and speaks in my ear. "But if you even *think* about safe-wording me within the next two hours, your car is mine, and you'll have no fucking chance of getting it back. Ever. Understand?"

I exchange a freaked-out look with Tanja on the bed. Clasping her fingers in her lap, she appears uncomfortable, too—for my sake, at least. Sebastian's a bastard that I want to punch in the face. But I need my car back! So, I shut my mouth and give a terse nod.

"Very well." His warm breath leaves my ear with a tingle before he inches away. "And now... Your hands, Raffael."

My gulp echoes through the room. Two shaky breaths later, I move my arms behind my back.

CHAPTER 6

Sebastian

As the seductive music fills the playroom, I take my time tying Raffael's hands with the black satin band. Once they're secured with a knot that I can loosen anytime with just a quick tug of one end, I run my fingertips down his open palm. His hand twitches. Oh so shy.

"Relax. I promise you'll enjoy this," I purr into his ear, aware of how fast his chest rises and falls with his breaths.

"Yeah, I doubt that," he growls. It's okay. He'll find out soon enough.

With my foot, I knock his legs apart so he stands

in a slight straddle before me. "Tanja, darling, would you come and aid me a little?" I keep my voice low and husky. She'll be the key tonight. The one who'll ease him into it—and the one who'll give him hell.

Like the innocent schoolgirl she resembles, she gets up from the bed and meets my gaze over Raffael's shoulder. "What do you want me to do?"

It was a good idea to come here a bit earlier and wait for her outside the building. Kidnapping her to the café down the street gave us some time to get acquainted with each other, and gave me a chance to get a feel for her. She's a friendly, open girl who knows how to take orders, not just in a fuck room like this. When she told me about her friendship with the two guys, especially with Raffael, I knew that she was just right for what I had in mind. What I'd wanted from the beginning.

"Would you get down on your knees for your friend?" My words come with a smile, but she doesn't miss the command in them. And neither does Raff. He sucks in a sharp breath but knows better than to protest. "Do a nice little job for him," I prompt Tanja.

She blinks, her uncertain gaze moving to Raffael's face. "*Go ahead,*" he mouths, but I know it takes a lot for him to do it. Two seconds later, the girl sinks to the floor before him and starts unbuttoning his jeans. Reaching around Raffael, I take her hands and move them away from his fly. Instead, I shove them around and place them on the back of his thighs, just under his butt. With Tanja's hands as a barrier between my body and his, I slowly move them upward, exploring him, yet giving him the sense of security that it's really his friend feeling him up. We have time. No need to overwhelm him in the first three minutes.

Breathing fast and staring straight out the window, Raffael doesn't move an inch. A muscle jumps in his jaw. I bring my mouth to his cheek, feeling the tic beneath my lips.

Tanja's fingers easily follow my directive when I let our joined hands wander to Raffael's front again. Together, we stroke his outer thighs moving to the inside, and then I let her hands roam upward, over his crotch. Even through her tender fingers, I can feel the bulge hardening beneath his jeans. He isn't entirely disinclined to the concept of what we're doing. That's good to see.

"Three days ago, you told me this room is for experiments," I whisper against the corner of his mouth, looking into his eyes from the side. "So, why do you fight it so hard?"

Only his eyes move to me, his gaze locking with mine as he swallows.

I leave Tanja's hands alone and open the fly of his jeans, peeling the two sides apart, giving his rigid cock some room. It's painful to be trapped inside too-tight jeans. I would know. I start feeling it myself, but I keep my own zipper closed for now.

"He's all yours," I rasp, casting a glance down at Tanja, who kneels like the nicest girl at school, perfectly in position. When I look into Raffael's face again, his eyes are closed, his features hard as granite.

I sit down on the bed's edge, reclining on my elbows with my feet still on the floor. From here, I watch Tanja hook her fingers in his tight, black boxer briefs and pull them down just enough to expose him entirely. She leaves her hands there and only brings her mouth to the tip of his beautiful erection. Raffael's chest visibly stills at the first touch of her tongue. Oh, yeah, we're getting closer to his limits. Or so he thinks. Because he doesn't yet know what's still ahead.

I give Tanja several minutes to lick and tease, but that she doesn't move her hands away from his hips raises my concern. After some time, I slide from the mattress and hunker behind her, opening the two buttons that hold her wrap-around skirt in place. I take it off and fling it aside, making short work of her bandeau top next, exposing her petite breasts. When she kneels there in nothing but a tiny lacy slip and black leather boots, I put my mouth to her temple and speak with a dark edge. "I'm sure he'll appreciate a little handwork, too, darling."

The shiver of unease that visibly runs through her when she tilts her head to me confuses me even more. "He—" She clears her throat, but her words don't become any louder. "He never lets me touch him."

Down there, is how her eyes finish the sentence.

"Oh, doesn't he?" When I look up, I find Raffael following our little chat with open eyes. I hold his deadly glare as I rise. Then I step behind him once more. My next words are so low beside his ear that one could almost call the conversation private. "Why is that, Raff? Do you not like being touched...*by a girl?*" I close my eyes, drawing in the scent of his fresh skin. Damn, he smells like the fucking glacier he always appears to be. Silent snow falling. I want to eat this guy up, from his tiny toe right to the perfect bow of his upper lip.

"You're an intriguing puzzle, Raffael," I say a little louder, letting Tanja in on my thoughts again. "Let's see if we can get all the pieces together before the night is over." Reaching down, I plant two fingers on each of Tanja's hands and move them right to the place where she should give Raff a little massage. Then I lift her chin with one finger and wink with a wicked grin. "Do me proud."

While she leans forward to work the icicle again in a way that costs him, a low moan forms deep in his throat. Ah, God, it reminds me of how much my cock demands attention. But tonight is not about me.

"Don't you dare come yet," I warn Raffael, almost chuckling next to his face. That would be too easy.

And we're not nearly done yet. "If you want your car back, you'll come when I tell you. Understand?"

His body tenses, but he refuses to answer me.

"I can't hear you, Raffael," I tease. "Do. You. Understand?"

Another moment ticks by before a very raspy, "*Yes*" scrapes out from his throat. It makes me smile.

Reaching to the front, I undo the top button of his white shirt. And the second. And the third.

With my lips brushing the crook of his neck, I pull the collar aside and down his shoulder. My tongue slips out, catching a taste of him. Boy, so delicious. I let my tongue run in hard circles over the sensitive spot on the side of his throat and finish unbuttoning his shirt. When the fabric falls open, I let my flat palms roam up over his hard abs and pecs, feeling every inch of him. His skin is smooth and incredibly hot. Is the iceberg finally melting? Could this be?

His nipples are pert like crystal grains beneath my hands. A very low, soft little moan sounds next to my ear. Oh, he's so good at suppressing. I push myself against his back, allowing him to lean against me when it appears his knees start to buckle a little at the seductive treatment he's getting from two sides. And he accepts. His head falls back on my shoulder as he furiously snaps his eyes shut, panting, and I wrap my arms around him to support his weight. My right hand splays over his chest, and I feel the anxious and excited drum of his heart underneath. "So fast..." I whisper as I nibble a path up his throat to his earlobe and give it a gentle bite. His breathing increases more, becoming almost labored. "Not yet, Raffael," I red-flag him in a daring, calm voice, then I tenderly lick the spot behind his ear. He swallows hard, and I almost have mercy. Almost.

"Tanja—" he croaks. "Please— Slow..."

Immediately, I feel her easing her rhythm. I cast a warning glare down at her over Raff's shoulder. "Do that, and you won't be able to sit for the entire next week!" Sure, I'd said I wouldn't spank a woman, but in this situation, even I could make an exception and give her the swatting of her life.

It's good to see that she doesn't doubt my words and resumes the way I want her to. Raffael's arousal is building up fast now. Sweat beads below his hairline, and I can feel the tiny twitches of his muscles when he struggles so hard to keep control in my embrace.

Sliding my hand up his throat to right under his chin, I turn his head, waiting for him to open his eyes and look at me. When he finally does, a longing spark ignites there that beckons me closer until I brush my lips across the corner of his mouth. But I'm not going to kiss him. Not tonight, and not under these circumstances. Even though I can feel the fire within him, the secret desire that just started to finally burn its way to the surface, he shall be the one deciding when our next kiss happens. And it *will* happen. He knows it as well as I. Because, right now, he's breathing for it. For me. The girl in front of him is utterly forgotten.

I bring both my hands down between us, tugging at the rope's end, releasing him from the ties. The band falls to the floor, his shirt slides down his arms, and his fingers slide between mine without me giving any orders this time. A simple caress was enough to coax his surrender. And I hold him tight.

Still stuck in the sleeves of his shirt, his arms

won't go all the way around to the front when I move them, so I let go just briefly to get rid of the garment, and let him find my hands again. Then I lift both our arms and bring them around him in an intimate embrace. He can close his eyes all he wants, it won't make the truth of this any less real.

My picture of Raffael becomes ever clearer, but some pieces still don't make sense. "Tanja?" I say softly, breaking through the trance-like music directing the beat of our hearts. "What does he usually prefer you to wear when he plays with you in this room? Other than ropes, I mean."

She lets go of Raffael's cock and fixes me with unsure eyes.

"Some lace? Kinky underwear? Nothing at all?" I list a few things that I fancy. But she startles me when she slowly shakes her head.

"No...?" I kiss Raffael's throat but keep my eyes trained on her. "Then what?"

Her voice holds a shy tremor when she tells me, "He likes it when I wear his t-shirts."

"Oh, fuck!" A disbelieving laugh breaks out of me as I finally piece the whole puzzle together and glance at Raffael. "You can't even look at them while you screw them, can you?"

In his glittering eyes, it's so obvious that even just me *knowing* it pains him. Deeply. It shouldn't. Nothing of this should hurt him. Ever.

I run my thumb across the back of his hand that is still in mine, but then my compassionate gaze returns to Tanja. "I assure you this has nothing to do with you personally. You have a stunning body, darling."

Still...I let go of Raffael and yank off my dark blue t-shirt, then toss it down into Tanja's lap. "Would you put that on, please?"

With deep concern in her doe eyes, she follows my command, while Raffael uses the time when neither hands nor a delicious mouth is on his cock to take a breath. His granted break is short, however. One look from me is enough, and Tanja gets back to working him with her mouth as viciously as before.

Feeling Raffael's warm back against my chest now, I grab his hands and slide them into his jeans' pockets with my own, digging our joined fingers against his groin.

"Why are you doing this?" he hoarsely pleads with me, squeezing his eyes tight to escape the world that so desperately wants to suck him in. For years, I believe.

"To prove you wrong."

"About what?"

I let my fingers glide out of his pockets and up his arms, whispering truthfully, "About everything you've made yourself believe your entire life."

Then I thread my arms through his and let my hands roam down from his belly button to the root of his erection. I don't get any closer because he pulls his hands out of his pockets and smacks them over mine, stopping me. I accept that. Sort of. He didn't safe-word me, but I sense that this is the last boundary he'll be able to cross tonight. And he's doing really well. Better than I thought at the beginning. And certainly better than he ever dared to believe I'm sure.

Slow enough to prepare him for the last hurdle tonight, I slide my hands out from under his and then gently lay them on top. This way, I move them down to replace Tanja's deft fingers encircling his cock. The moan that follows is heart-wrenching. And cock-stirring. Fuck, if I just rub my crotch against him for a second, I'm going to come in my pants like a prepubescent boy.

Not going to happen. Not in front of the girl. She came here with expectations, and someone's got to fulfill those. To have two guys coming outside her would be selfish and certainly a bit discouraging.

But not to overburden Raffael with the intensity of this whole new situation, I just let him work himself for half a minute under my fingers, then I move our hands away, stretching his arms to the back and letting Tanja take over for the finish. "You can come now, if you want," I rasp into his ear, barely having a voice myself anymore.

It takes exactly three seconds until he digs his fingers hard into the sides of my thighs and presses himself against me, coming undone in Tanja's mouth. When I push my hands into his front pockets and just do a little stroking there, he leans his head against my shoulder and finally gives up trying to keep control. I kiss and tease the bend of his neck with my tongue all the way through his climax, enjoying his shattering little moans.

Tanja is gorgeous. She sucks him completely dry before she wipes her mouth with two fingers and then gently buttons him up again.

Once I'm certain that Raffael can stand without my support, I draw away from him and give Tanja a smile, crooking my finger to make her stand up. I grab the hem of my t-shirt and slowly pull it over her head as she raises her arms. Then I kiss her on the cheek and softly say, "Would you wait on the bed for me?"

While she nods and sits down on the purple sheets, I turn around, directing my smile at Raffael now. He slipped into his white shirt but left it unbuttoned. "Did you enjoy that?" I ask him, leaning my back against the bedpost, and balling up my t-shirt in my hands.

"Like a root canal," he growls, but his gleaming eyes tell a different story.

"Oh, come on, pretty snowflake. Don't gimme that shit." I fling my t-shirt aside and step up to him until I'm in his face. "I could have made you come without your friend's mouth on you. And faster, too.

And you know it. You enjoyed every fucking stroke of your skin."

I can see the change in his eyes when he finally finds his composure again. His gaze turns air to ice around us now that no one's sucking his cock anymore. "The only reason I let you touch me is because I want my car back. And you made it the condition, asshole. This had nothing to do with joy. Not in the least."

I sigh. "Ah, Raffael... I really wish you'd have said something else."

"Like?" He lifts an eyebrow.

"The truth."

Stubbornly, he folds his arms over his naked chest under the open shirt. "And you think the truth is that I could be attracted to you in any freaking way?"

"To admit that"—I mirror his bearing—"would be a great start, actually."

He tilts his head with a cynical half-smile that stops way short of anywhere near his eyes. "Sorry to bust your illusions, but I'm not."

"Sorry to bust *yours*, Raff, but you *are*." Kudos for his unwavering glare into my eyes, though. Most people, when called out on being gay, wouldn't be able to control their look of acute panic and embarrassment. He's obviously been keeping a lock on this part of himself for a very long time. The control shit makes more and more sense. "I wish you could accept it and just let go. For your sake, not for mine."

Okay, for mine, too. I really, *really* want to fuck this guy because he's possibly the hottest thing I've laid eyes on in the past couple of years. And if we don't make good progress here soon, I'll have to use more direct ways to open his eyes. They can be quite painful, and there, I wouldn't have to touch him at all.

"I don't care for this stupid conversation." His eyes narrow to cold slits. "Do you want to hand fuck me again, or was this enough to get my car back?"

"I believe I have another hour before my time here is over," I retort with the same frostiness. But I'm not a sadist like he is with his submissives. Nothing of what *I* just did was to kill a longing inside me that I cannot cope with—like I suspect is the case with him. I'd rather teach him a particular lesson.

Something about himself. I only wish it wasn't so hard for him to accept the truth. And I'm not at all sure whether he can stomach it on top of everything else tonight. Fingers slipping into my pockets, I let my tongue run across my upper teeth before sucking on my left canine. "But I'll make you a fair offer."

"What?"

"Kiss me, and you can leave the room now."

Stepping back, he expels an incredulous laugh. "You're mental if you think for one moment—"

"Last chance, Raffael," I interrupt. And I mean it.

He leans against the chest of drawers, gripping the edge with both hands so hard that his knuckles turn white. "I'm not going to kiss you. And I'm *certainly* not going to leave you alone in here with her." He nods toward the bed where Tanja still sits, hugging her booted legs to her chest, watching us silently like the most obedient girl in the world. He trained her well.

"If you're scared I'll hurt her, I can assure you that she'll enjoy every minute of her time with me. But you should take this warning seriously, Raffael. Her pleasure will be your pain."

He says nothing, just dares me with one arched eyebrow. And I sigh.

"Very well." I grab his arm and haul him across the room, cursing his stubborn ignorance. The padded manacles coming down from the cross-piece at the side of the bed have tempted me from the moment I first set foot in this room three days ago. It's time to give them a try at last.

I have Raffael kneel on the bed and lift his arms so I can cuff both wrists, all the while breathing in his Arctic snow scent. The manacles are clearly positioned for Tanja's height, leaving Raffael far too much room. At the headboard, I find the mechanism to adjust the chains and give them a hard pull until he hangs in the manacles like he's crucified.

Beautiful.

I grab his chin and force him to look at me. "This time, I'm not going to touch you. But what comes now might hurt you more than what we did before. Don't say later that I didn't warn you."

"Go to hell," he replies with death in his voice.

Oh, yes. I think he just got a pretty good idea of what he's going to face.

CHAPTER 7

Raffael

My body is still on fire, my mind is reeling, and my arms start to turn numb. Sebastian tightened the chains too much where I'm suspended from the top of the bed, kneeling on the mattress. I'm hanging at his mercy, with a front-row seat to a fuck I really don't want to watch.

Tanja lies sprawled on the sheets before me, tilting her head back and looking up at me. "*You okay?*" she mouths quickly while Sebastian skirts the bed to stand between her legs across from me. Lips compressed, I assure her with a curt nod. She doesn't need to know how the past hour shattered my insides and left me in pieces.

Sebastian's muscles on his arms and back bulge as he leans over Tanja's naked body. The tattoos that run across his firm chest wander onto his biceps and then farther down his right arm. I concentrate on the black leather bracelet that sits on his left wrist where his watch should be, as he bends his head down and drawls in her ear, "Shall we test how long *you* last if I don't allow you to come, darling?"

Her face flushed, she bites her bottom lip and gives a tiny nod.

Sebastian glides down her body, brushing his lips in a straight line over her skin, dragging her slip down her thighs on the way. "It's gift-unwrapping-day," he breathes with pleasure against her waxed pussy but doesn't linger there. With her panties gone, he gently spreads her knees a little, then lifts her right leg and unzips the black leather boot. Very slowly, he slides it off her foot, then drops it to the floor and starts kissing a trail from her ankle up along the inside of her calf and thigh, keeping his gaze trained on her face. But when he plants the first real kiss to her glistening core, his eyes find mine, and he fixes me with a wicked little grin.

I hold his stare, not even blinking. Only when he dedicates his attention to the girl beneath him again, I close my eyes, gripping the chains above the padded shackles harder. Moments later, the sound of the second boot being abandoned drifts to me, followed by tiny moans from Tanja. I know her scale, know what every little sound of hers means. I know the tiny squeaks when she gets tickled in certain places, and all the raspy groans when she falls into deeper passion, longing for release.

And from what I hear, Sebastian is doing a good job of pleasuring her.

Jesus Christ, let me fall unconscious, please!

One sheep. Two sheep. Three sheep...

I wish I could tune out the sounds. And the pictures they're painting in my head without me even looking. Damn Sebastian. Damn him to hell for playing this evil game with me.

Twenty-four. Twenty-five. Twenty-six. Twenty-seven...

All I can do is try to convince myself that it's Felix pleasuring Tanja before me. Because any other thought hurts like hell.

One thousand two hundred and ninety. One thousand two hundred and ninety-one. One thousand two hundred and ninety-two.

"Raffael?" Sebastian's soft but demanding voice strokes over my skin and leaves me in tremors. "Open your eyes."

I know I don't have a choice. I've come so far. I only need to endure a few more minutes to finally get what I want. What I *really* want. The *only* thing I want. My car. Not this fucking asshole in front of me.

Swallowing hard, I do as he says. And immediately wish I hadn't. He kneels in front of me, buck-naked, fully erect—and holds a fucking condom packet in front of my lips. "Would you open this for me, please?"

One thousand two hundred and ninety-three.

I place my teeth around the corner and tear the foil open by slowly turning my head.

One thousand two hundred and ninety-four.

Then I glare into his eyes and spit the ripped-off bit into his face.

One thousand two hundred and ninety-five.

He blows out a quiet laugh and whispers, "No closing your eyes again."

Whatever sadistic ideas he has, I refuse to watch him slip the condom over his cock and instead let my gaze fall on Tanja's porcelain face. Her eyes are closed, and the blush on her cheeks indicates that she's already been through her first orgasm. As if I hadn't noticed that by her whimpering at eight hundred and forty-seven sheep.

Sebastian moves into my line of vision again as he braces himself over her. Tanja opens her eyes with a smile. Her legs jerk a little around his waist as he slides into her and then begins to rock in a gentle pace that makes the muscles in his perfect butt twitch in a hypnotic rhythm. Fucking hell, I realize much too late how long I've been staring and move my gaze up over his well-defined back and shoulders. His dark hair hangs in sweaty strands across his forehead. His breathing is slow but intense, and all the while he moves inside Tanja, his eyes fix mine with a passion that scares me.

Getting closer to another climax, Tanja brings her

hands to his back, digging her nails into his shoulder blades, but he's fast to move them away. Gripping her left hand tightly, he kisses the pads of her fingertips and looks down at her face for the first time in minutes. "No scratches, darling," he whispers and smiles.

Just when I think the worst part of my torture tonight lies behind me, my heart stops beating when he leans down to kiss her on her mouth. He opens her lips with his and slides his tongue inside. I let my head fall back and stare at the ceiling, clenching my teeth.

He said to keep my eyes open, not that I had to watch.

One. Million. Sheep.

I make them all run over me and kill me in my thoughts.

Because...yes, goddammit, Sebastian was right. His fingers sliding over my body did something to me. I cannot tell what it was. I don't even want to go there and explore it because it means having to deal with demons I'm not ready to face. But if he had kissed me half an hour ago when his arms were still wrapped around me in a masterful embrace, I would have let him. And liked it.

Staring at the chains running along the cross-piece of the bed, I bite my bottom lip until I taste blood. I've been screwing girls since I was sixteen. How the hell can I possibly be attracted to a man now?

A touch on my left hand rips me out of my thoughts, and my head jerks to the side. Sebastian, dressed in his dark blue t-shirt and jeans again, unbuckles the manacles around my wrists. He's quiet, his expression soft. Standing by the door fully dressed, Tanja looks at me in silent compassion for what I had to go through. Then she leaves us alone.

I snort and swallow, rubbing my wrists once I'm free and can get off the bed. "Are we done?" I ask, my tone ice-cold.

Sebastian nods.

"The Corvette is mine again, and nothing will change that?"

He slips his hand into his jeans' pocket and retrieves the car key, holding it out to me on his open palm. Grinding my teeth, I grab it. I look at it for a short, intense moment, then I fist my fingers around it and land an iron-hard punch on his jaw. His head snaps to the side, and he grabs the bedpost as he stumbles. "You fucking asshole!" I spit.

This is the first time I've ever hit a man. And the sting in my hand is one I don't recognize. But the pain feels good in a strange way. It's welcome. It drowns out thoughts I don't want to have. It's a thousand times better than counting goddamned sheep.

As Sebastian straightens again, he runs the tip of his tongue over the corner of his mouth, licking at the blood there. Then he wipes the rest away with the back of his hand. "Feel better?"

"Yes." And no. And... *argh, God save the queen!*

"Good. Now, sit."

I laugh. A sound full of venom. "You don't give me any more orders in this room."

Sebastian just rolls his eyes. "Please... Sit down." His gaze briefly switches to the edge of the bed. There's an honest softness in his eyes that makes me want to follow his...request. It wasn't an order.

Sitting actually feels good after all the time spent on my knees. I get a chance to catch my breath.

He grabs the lounge chair by the armrest and pulls it closer, taking a seat right in front of me. With his forearms braced on his knees and his fingers laced, he leans forward a little to look me straight in the eyes for a long, fathomless moment. When he finally starts to speak, he sounds completely different from how he behaved the entire night. Calm. Grown-up. Experienced. All the things I don't feel. "You are who you are, Raffael. And it's not going to go away, no matter how often you punish Tanja—or any other woman—for it."

My throat feels so tight, I don't think I can even swallow the spit in my mouth.

"And once you're ready to accept that," he continues, giving me a hint of a warm smile that reaches his eyes, "I'd love to see you again."

Inhale. Exhale. I tip backward on the sheets because I don't know what else to do right now. Sebastian laughs. Then he gets up and pats my right thigh, just once. "You have my number." A moment after he leaves the room, and I hear the bathroom door falling shut.

Jesus Christ. I rub my hands over my face and

groan. What a fucking mess!

While Sebastian is obviously cleaning himself up after the intense time the three of us just had in the playroom, I climb off the bed and trudge downstairs. Tanja sits on the couch, watching my every move. She must have been to my room because she's wearing one of my black hoodies over her outfit now. She remains silent. I assume we'll talk soon. Once we're alone.

For now, I get the key to the Honda from the kitchen island where I put it this afternoon and turn around when I hear Sebastian jogging down the stairs. He casts me a flirtatious glance, but it's clear that he won't say another word tonight. Not to me anyway. Instead, he crosses to Tanja, places his hand on her neck, and pulls her slightly forward to press a kiss to the top of her head. "Thanks for your help, darling," he tells her.

As he heads for the door, I toss his key across the room, and he catches it with one hand. Lips compressed in a tiny smile, he lifts his eyebrows once as a goodbye—or a promise, I'm not sure which. Then he leaves my apartment, and the door slams shut.

I stare at the closed portal for one more minute, then head back into the kitchen to grab a bottle of water from the fridge. Unscrewing the cap, I take a deep draught, not ready to face Tanja yet. Or hear what she has to say.

For a long time, I glare into the open bottle, trying to find some fucking answers in the beverage. But water is always silent, no matter how shallow or deep. Eventually, I screw the top back on and grip the bottle tightly as I slowly walk into the living room and lower to the couch across from Tanja. It takes another moment before I can bring myself to look into her eyes.

She sighs.

I sigh, too. And pull my legs up onto the couch.

I don't want to hear what she thinks. I don't want to read it in her eyes. Shit, I don't want to have this conversation at all.

But it continues...on and on.

She drags her bottom lip between her teeth.

I swallow.

Her blinks come steadily, though with incredibly

long periods of time between them.

I loop my arms around my legs and press my knees to my chest, gripping the water bottle tightly.

Tanja tilts her head, and I lean my forehead against my knees, burying my face in the blackness of the cave I created.

Something rustles on the couch. Gentle fingers unclench mine and take the bottle away from me. Then warm, female arms wrap around me and hold on tight.

Breathing hurts.

She strokes up and down my back.

I put down my feet and pull her sideways onto my lap. Pressing my face to the crook of her neck, I hug her hard, as if she were my teddy bear of comfort.

Her fingers skim through my hair. Then she presses her cheek against the top of my head and just holds me. "It's good the way it is," she whispers.

And I'm grateful for this conversation.

CHAPTER 8

Raffael

Tanja left, and for the last hour, I've just randomly zipped through the channels in hopes of finding something that could distract me. Somehow, I'm not up to meeting my friends online for some zombie killing tonight, although it probably would have been a better choice, considering what rubbish is on TV at half-past one in the morning.

I run through all one hundred and twenty channels one last time, not even trying to smother my wide yawn. Maybe it's time to just go to bed. But then my thumb hovers over the button to move on when a newscaster with black curls and a red blouse throws the words "*Gay Pride*" directly at me.

The term is responsible for an uncomfortable wave of adrenaline combusting through my body. Still, with narrowed eyes, I remain on BBC and listen to the news lady when she speaks about the approaching Gay Pride Parade in London the first week of July. I don't really know why I stop to hear what she has to say. Maybe it's because I like her voice. Or perhaps it's because some asshole with a white Honda fucked me into stranger worlds tonight.

The broadcast, a montage of parades all across England, captures partying people on camera. Some of them look normal, others are dressed in very flamboyant outfits. They laugh a lot. And they kiss even more. They actually look really happy.

The report continues with blends of opponents of that lifestyle marching in counter-demonstrations, with street fights breaking out. My gut churns. The news lady speaks about the riots to be expected again at the parade—like every other year before. I press the button to turn off this shit and head to bed. The last thing I want on my mind right now is the image of a group of assholes marching up because I kissed a man three days ago...and liked it.

Perhaps.

Or maybe not.

Agh, I don't know!

Okay, maybe just a little.

I rub my face and groan into my palms. Jesus Christ! What is happening with me?

*

It's the final week at university. All the exams are already over, and I only have three more courses this week. Two this morning, and the last one on Friday.

Tanja studies art at the same university where I undergo my architecture studies. It's nice to have her around where I can meet her at breaks. When we can, we pick up Felix for lunch from the airbrush shop where he works. So far, we barely left out two days in a row. This week, however, I use the excuse of not being at the campus to avoid my friends. I just don't feel like talking about what happened recently, and given the vow we took to never keep any secrets between us, I'm quite sure that Felix already knows how the two hours in my playroom spiraled terribly out of control.

I just need a little time to cope with everything and find my balance again.

Both of them talk to me through WhatsApp every day, though. Tanja more often than Felix, asking how I feel and if I want to talk about anything. I still don't. Not yet. What I want is to race my car up to the country and back and revel in the joy of having my baby to myself again. Sebastian put the papers in the glove compartment. I could have done the same with his, but I didn't. The ownership paperwork for the Honda still sits on my desk in the study, where I put it after Sebastian left with only the key. I ripped the contract into a million pieces and threw them in the trash, though.

On Thursday evening, my friends obviously decide that my break from seeing people is over and come by for a surprise visit. They're lucky I like them because I usually don't welcome people into my apartment if they don't notify me at least an hour before. My lips are compressed into a thin line as I pull open the door and meet their eyes.

It's one thing to deal with Tanja. I can make *her* shut up whenever I want. But I have no idea how Felix will react to the news of a guy dominating me in my own playroom. It's embarrassing to the bone.

The three of us stand there, confronting each other for three silent seconds. Until Felix finally lifts a white plastic bag with several boxes from the Chinese takeaway place we like and smirks, squeezing past me. "We brought food. Now, pick your pussy up from the floor and let us in. I'm hungry."

And that was that.

Tanja then stands on her tiptoes and kisses me on the cheek, whispering a soft, "Hi" into my ear.

I close the door and follow them, albeit a little reluctantly, into the living room, where I take a seat on the armrest of the couch as they unpack the steaming paper boxes with their spicy-smelling dishes. Tanja hands me a pair of chopsticks, and I slide from the armrest onto the cushions to reach for the container with the Peking roasted duck. Crossing my legs on the couch, I shovel the first bite into my mouth and only then realize that I haven't eaten anything in two full days. Man, this tastes delicious.

"So," Felix says around a bite and casts me a nonchalant glance, "how does it feel to have a man's hands on your body?"

Jesus Christ! I spit the chewed duck back into the box, nailing him with a shocked stare.

"Felix!" Tanja pokes him hard with her elbow, indignation clear on her face.

He stares as if his question were the most natural thing in the world, then just scrunches his face at her, looking all innocent. "Whaaat?"

My cheeks burn as if they were on fire.

"I—he—" She glares at him. "We're eating!" is her final excuse, which only makes Felix laugh. Me, too. A little.

"When Raff and I eat without you, we always discuss your pussy and how great you are to—"

"Feeelix..." Now it's my turn to shut him up.

Laughing, I head into the kitchen to remove the spat-out duck from the rest of my dinner and toss it into the garbage, but his protest of, "You two are no fun tonight," follows me, and makes me shake my head. When I return and continue eating what's left of the Peking duck, he finds a different subject. Thank God.

"Hey, you know that amazing guy from *Facelift Cars*? The one with the blue hair?"

"Yes," I mumble around my next bite. It's a show about pimping cars that's been running in the UK for years. Felix and I often watch it together.

"No," Tanja answers.

Of course.

Felix rolls his eyes at her and then keeps on speaking in my direction rather than hers. "He wants an airbrush painting for his car and came to the shop this morning. Diego is considering letting me do it because the guy liked my work best from our catalog of past projects."

"Wow." My eyes widen with surprise and honest admiration. "That's huge!"

He grins like a loon. "They even want to bring it on the show."

I'm incredibly proud of Felix. He deserves this. His work is exquisite. "What kind of motif does he want?"

"He fancied the face of a panther I did on a truck

once. Something like that, I'd guess. By the way—"
He points his chopsticks at me across the coffee table. "Do you already know what you want me to do on the Stingray?"

"I'm thinking about a smoky skull on the hood. And maybe a skeletal middle finger for the rear."

Rolling her eyes, Tanja deadpans, "Awesome."

"Hey, we cannot cover the Corvette in pixies, even if you'd love that, baby," Felix mocks her and bumps his shoulder into hers so she loses the chicken trapped between her chopsticks. While she fishes for it again, my WhatsApp beeps with a message. I stick my chopsticks into the box I'm still holding and, with my free hand, fetch my smartphone from my jeans' pocket.

As I unlock the display, however, my pulse jumps from sixty to two sixty in a nanosecond. All sounds die in the room as I'm staring dumbfounded at my phone.

I swallow.

"Okay, dude, we can hear your heart beating over here," Felix says a little nervously. "So either you won the lottery, or—"

"Sebastian sent you a message," Tanja finishes his sentence on a joyful breath.

I look up into her hopeful eyes, my lips still thinning.

Instantly, her smile gets wider. "What did he say?"

"Oh, come on," Felix moans at her. "Give the dude some privacy."

I usually don't mind Tanja's endless curiosity, but tonight, I actually appreciate Felix's intervention. It scares me to death that I only read his name on the display and not even the message itself yet, and still, something inside me goes crazy like I won a Lamborghini or something.

When I don't move for a lengthened breath, Felix starts to pack up the food and puts it back into the plastic bag. "It's late. We better leave."

"You want to do *what*?" Tanja's outraged protest is almost sweet as he takes the chopsticks out of her hands.

He tosses them into the bag, too. "Get up, Tanja."

"But why? It's so sweet, and I—"

Felix grabs her chin and makes her look up at him, standing above her. "Door! *Now!*" he commands and nails her with a glare that leaves no room for discussion. Whoa, even I feel the urge to rise and get my jacket to leave.

Tanja's eyes widen with surprise, then she gets up from the couch and follows him to the foyer. With me right behind her, she throws a glance over her shoulder, mouthing a confused *"What?"* at me. All I feel able to do is shrug. I haven't seen Felix like this before. But at least he's found the right tone with her to make her obey.

"We can finish eating at my place," he offers, just the slightest bit softer, yet still strict enough for her not to argue.

Tanja whirls around and kisses me goodbye on the cheek. "Call me later and tell me what he wanted," she whispers and grins before she slips out the door.

Felix claps his hand into mine. "We can speak about the airbrush painting tomorrow."

I nod. "Thanks for the food."

Then the door falls shut, and I'm alone.

I turn around to scowl at my phone on the coffee table ten feet away. Holy fuck. Something's seriously wrong with me if a tiny beep can break off a cozy dinner like that.

With my heart racing once more, I walk back into the living room and plant myself on the couch, finally opening the message.

Sebastian

You know that you only gave me the key and not the papers back, right?

I stare at the single line for a very long time, feeling a strange excitement at the slight provocation in the words. Now what? Start a conversation? Just tell him to come by tomorrow and pick them up? Shit, all of those thoughts are confusing. Most of all, the fact that I even have to think about it and not just reply like I normally would with any other person in the world.

I fold my hands over my mouth and nose and blow out a nervous breath. Then I type just a single word.

Me

Yes.

It takes three seconds until the two checks turn blue, and another ten until a new text pops up. All this time, my fingers cramp around the phone.

Sebastian

Planning to change that?

Oh boy, this means meeting again. Both excitement and a flood of fear swamp me. My mouth dries out.

Me

Yes.

Three dots doing the wave indicate that he's typing something again. Transfixed, I stare at them until they change to text.

Sebastian

Great. Is yes the only word your phone spits out?

He has me grinning with that, and I type just *yes* again. But then I delete it. That's stupid. Or is it?

After all, he walked into that one. While I type it again and delete it once more, the waving dots reappear. He's typing, too. His message comes in before I can send mine. Which I wouldn't have because I deleted it again.

Sebastian

Seriously, how many times did you type fucking YES now and delete it again?

I crack up laughing and then put three teary-laughing smiley faces before my answer.

Me

Too many times!!

Then I sink deeper into the couch, dip my head against the backrest, and grimace at the ceiling. My heart rate normalizes before his next message comes in, and I actually start to enjoy the conversation that grows a little faster from then on.

Sebastian

So... My papers, Raffael?

Me

I'll mail them to you.

Sebastian

Don't you fucking dare, snowflake...

Me

Hey! Easiest way.

Sebastian

The easiest way would be to meet me and hand them over.

I swallow at this obvious request. It wouldn't be the easiest way. If anything, it's the hardest way I can imagine. I take a long time to consider how to ease out of this.

Me

Sorry, I have a really busy week. I can't.

Sebastian

Coward

Me

I'm not. It's true. Lots of uni stuff to do.

Sebastian

Your final week before the summer? I've been to college, too. I know how it goes.

I bite my bottom lip.

Fuck.

There's probably no easy way out of this. But the last thing I want is Sebastian in my apartment again. So I sigh and suggest the café where Tanja told me the two of them went before that fatal night in the playroom.

Me

Fine. Meet at Starbucks down the road?

Sunday at 4 pm.

Sebastian

FRIDAY at 4 pm. Good night, Raff.

Shit! I gulp. Friday is tomorrow.

CHAPTER 9

Sebastian

I arrive at Starbucks late. The traffic was murder, and then I had to walk two blocks from the parking lot to the café. It would probably have been a better idea to park in the underground car park at Raffael's apartment building. Would have saved me fifteen minutes for sure.

Flipping the bill of my black Nike ball cap to the back of my head, I push open the door and scan the place. When I spot a familiar face at a table in the rear, I chuckle and shake my head. What a fucking chicken. Heading straight to the booth where my car papers wait for me, I slide in next to the black-haired girl and fold my arms provocatively across the table opposite Raffael. "Seriously? You had to bring backup?" I tease him. "Scared it could look too much like a date if you came alone?"

His tight answering smile is cute.

I reach over, slide my fingers around the girl's neck, and pull her closer for a kiss on her head. "Hi, Tanja."

The waitress comes by, and I order an espresso with a glass of water. "And whatever she wants," I add with a nod at Tanja since her cup is empty.

"A caramel frappuccino, please," she says, smiling.

Silence ensues after the waitress leaves. I merely play the eyeing game with Raff. His lips tighten, and I want to laugh. When the woman comes back with our drinks, I pay for both of them straight away as is customary in this shop. I would have offered the snowflake a drink, too, but his iced coffee is still half-full. The girl obviously sucks a bit faster than he does.

"You're lucky she's with me and stopped me from leaving with your papers ten minutes ago," Raffael says, picking up my earlier jibe and sounding a lot more like himself than the last time we met. Well, at least a lot more like the guy I first got to know on the night of the race. He picks up a small stack of papers from the place next to him and pushes them in front of me, adding, "I *reeeally* hate it when people are late."

At his words, I tilt my head. He said it in such a way that it makes me believe I should take it as a serious warning if I want to hang out with him some more. And I do. So, I just hold his gaze with a warm expression, no bantering this time, and give a short nod in agreement. "I'll be more considerate around you in the future."

My comeback wipes Raffael's grin right off his face. A thin layer of goosebumps coat the skin of his forearms right up to the pushed-back sleeves of his oversized white hockey shirt. His brow furrows with some confusion, and Tanja laughs. "You're incredibly sweet when someone surprises you, Raff, you know that?" she tells her friend and spoons the whipped cream of her drink into her mouth.

"Like a shy little snowflake," I agree with a smirk, folding my arms on the table, and winking at Raffael.

As if in a panic that someone could have seen, his gaze darts around the place for a moment. The next, he quickly lowers his face to hide his eyes behind the thatch of platinum blond hair falling across his brow as he stares into his drink. "Jesus Christ! Could you please not flirt with me here?" he mutters.

To get his attention back, I reach for his cup and pull it away from him. His gaze tracks my hand, but it stops at my face. "Okay," I drawl without smiling, my voice holding a notch of provocation this time. "Then where?"

His Arctic blue eyes fix on me, a million emotions flashing in them. Shock is the most evident, but there's also curiosity. Desire. And when he seems to realize his thoughts, a tiny blush blossoms across the upper third of his cheeks. Just a breath of red, really. It's adorable.

That he won't give me an answer becomes clear when he makes a grab for his iced coffee and pulls it back, teeth clenched. But a surprising suggestion comes from the girl next to me. "Playroom," Tanja says.

We both turn to her, and Raffael blurts out an

incredulous, "What?"

She gives a nonchalant shrug as if those thirty square meters in his apartment could save all the tiny problems in the world. "Sorry." Focus still on spooning her frappuccino, she murmurs, "Ignore me. I was just thinking out loud."

I tilt my head, not intending for one minute to let this idea slip away. "No. Speak on, please." She has me all curious now.

Prompted by my words, she looks up and clears her throat. "Well..." Her gaze wanders back and forth between Raffael and me, but it remains on him for a moment longer, and her next words are addressed to him alone. "It's kind of obvious that you...find the idea of getting to know Sebastian better...intriguing." She grimaces, and her face brightens with a blush of unease because she's making her friend uncomfortable right now, and she knows it.

I, however, like her word choice.

Her dark eyes move back to me as she expels a long breath. "You made him question a few things about who he is, and he likely needs time to adjust to this whole new side of himself."

Touched by her words, I cut a brief glance at Raffael, who will doubtlessly crack his molars any second now if he grinds his teeth any harder.

"The playroom has always been a place sort of outside this world," Tanja explains to me then. "Different rules. Nothing that touches real life if you don't want it to. A room where anything is possible. I think it's a good place for you to start if you want to spend more time with Raff. No dominant or submissive there this time. Just the two of you as you are. I know that he'll appreciate it, even if he won't speak a word to me ever again just for saying this."

"You're so right about that," comes the deadly snarl from across the table. I briefly feel the need to throw myself in the line of fire to stop his ice-cold glare from killing the girl.

"Oh come on, Raff, please." She places her hand on his, but he jerks it away. "You've done crazier things in life than stretching your sexuality, and you're still breathing. So why don't you just give this thing a chance? I know that Sebastian wants this. He told me so on Monday before we came to your place.

And I know you want it, too. Somehow. Deep down inside you."

Probably beneath all the shitty rules he holds himself to.

It doesn't feel right to say something now because this seems to be a conversation between the two of them, and I have to accept whatever the outcome is. But when Raffael wraps his fingers so tightly around his glass that I fear he'll break it, my chest constricts a little for him.

"I—*can't*." With his gaze on the table, the two words wrench from his throat. It must cost him immensely to even speak with us right now.

"Sure, you can," Tanja assures him softly as if he were a child she wants to get through to. "Don't look at this as a life-altering experience. Maybe more like an experiment in a...chemistry laboratory. You go there, you try things, you see if the result is something you can work with, and if not, you leave and close the door on it."

"Right. And if you mix things in there that just aren't compatible, you blow up the whole place," he snaps. "And you don't just close doors on *that*, you know."

So much fear.

Inhaling deeply, I lick my lips. It must be painful to get crushed by so many new emotions. I figured out pretty early that I fancied boys, it wasn't such a shattering realization for me. But at twenty-three years old and after screwing girls for half his life, this must be hard to accept. Since silence has fallen upon the table, I chance a brief brush of my knuckles across the backs of his fingers. "I won't bust your apartment, I promise."

Raffael moves his hands with the glass away, but not as jerkily this time as he did earlier when Tanja touched him. Still, he squeezes his eyes shut as if he wants nothing more than to just lock himself up in a place far, far away from this new reality he has yet to learn to cope with.

His nostrils flare with quickened breaths. I reckon he'll shoot me a glare like deadly lasers any moment and send me straight to hell. Instead, he surprises not only me but also Tanja when he suddenly rises from the table. Without a single word of goodbye to his friend or me, he leaves the café and heads outside, moving off in the direction of his apartment.

I drop my forehead to my folded arms and murmur against the wooden surface of the table, "Fantastic."

Next to me, Tanja sighs. If I didn't block her way out of the booth, I imagine she'd be dashing after Raffael now. "Please, don't give up just yet," she begs me quietly. I'm not sure what exactly she even means by it. Giving up on easing Raffael into a world where it's possible that a guy likes a guy? Or giving up on trying to get closer to him? Because she knows I want both.

We had a very long and really nice chat about Raffael the last time we sat here, and I told her then that it's been a while since I was attracted to someone as intensely as I am to Raff. From the very first moment I laid eyes on him. It might be because our entire acquaintance kind of started in reverse with a really nice kiss—one that I couldn't get out of my mind for days. But there's just something to the guy that keeps me wanting to be around him more than I probably should. His entire bearing. Especially his rough walls. I want to rip them down and find out what's behind them. Because I'm sure what's hiding there is amazing. But...

"Iceland titanium is hard to crack," I whine.

Tanja chuckles. "If you want to get through to him, then now is the best possible moment." She slides the cap off my head, and I tilt my face sideways, bedding my cheek on my arms to look at her. Her dark eyes gleam with hope. "I know he'll be pacing his apartment over the next few hours, like a tiger in a cage. You shifted his world off its axis. Now do something about it. Don't give him time to rebuild his walls." She sets the cap down on the table so the Nike label faces me. I read the tiny words beneath.

Do it!

"Tomorrow, it'll be too late," she says softly. Then she noisily slurps the rest of her caramel frappuccino through the straw and licks her lips with a loud smack.

I guess that was the end of her speech. And she gave me a lot to think about. After emptying my own cup, I put my hat on again and get out of the booth. The rolled-up papers to my car go into my back pocket.

We leave Starbucks together. "Want me to drive you home? My car's parked a couple of blocks from here," I offer when we get outside.

Tanja's long, black hair flies when she shakes her head, and she flashes me an honest smile. "No, thanks. I love riding the bus. And you have other things to do now."

I nod, grateful for her help with Raffael once again, and head in the opposite direction as she does. After a few steps, though, I stop and turn back to her. "Tanja!" When she spins around, almost at the corner of the street, I ask, "What do you and Felix do when you want to get him a little bit farther out of his comfort zone?"

Her eyes thoughtfully narrowed, Tanja takes a second to consider. Then she looks up and shrugs. "Simple." Her lips spread into a wide grin. "We dare him."

She waves and hurries on to the bus station. I start off, too, to find the Honda.

Dare him... The thought circles in my mind the entire time I walk the two blocks. It was a dare that got Raffael's cute ass in trouble in the first place, and I saved him that night with a kiss. But how does that fit into his scheme of keeping control over everything at all times? Of living by such strict rules? Why would he get himself into precarious situations if it's so against his principles?

The answer escapes me.

Ten feet away from the Honda, I unlock the doors and slide in behind the wheel, tossing the car's papers onto the passenger seat. The belt harness presses into my back. I don't want to put it on right now. I don't want to start the engine either because I don't want to go home. But what other choice do I have? It's hardly a good idea to drive back to Brook's Mew and ring Raffael down from his apartment to talk. Half an hour ago, he made it clear that he isn't up for talking.

Tanja, on the other hand, said I shouldn't wait until tomorrow. And she knows him a lot better than I do.

Gripping the steering wheel, I bang my head against it. Fuck if I'm not caught between a rock and a hard place right now.

After a long, deep sigh, I lift my head and reach for the start button, but then my finger hovers. Seconds stretch on. Eventually, I lean back, engine still cold, and bite my lip while I stare out the windshield. Perhaps hovering is the best thing I can actually do right now.

I pull out my phone and open the thread of my last WhatsApp chat with Iceland. One deep breath later, I type a message and press send.

Me

No ties.

He reads the text seconds later, but it takes him at least five minutes to reply.

Iceland

What?

Me

In your playroom. I like Tanja's idea. We can do this differently, after all. No bondage. No dominance. Just talking for a start.

144

Iceland

We talked at the café.

Me

No, we didn't. You shut off. Iceland closed the borders...

Iceland

Give me a minute to breathe.

Me

I am. I understand that you're not yet ready to sit with a guy in public.

Iceland

Why do you think that?

Me

You kept scanning the place, making sure no one saw me wink at you. Or touch you. Or do anything that could lead them to think that you and I might have something going.

Iceland

Because we don't.

Me

Right.

I send off the last message, then drop my hand with the phone and rub my face with the other. I know that he won't reply if I leave it like that. And it would be such a shame. Because even sending texts back and forth with Raffael gives me a good feeling. And I bet it does for him, too.

So I scoot deeper into the seat, jam my lifted knee against the steering wheel, and write to him once more.

Me

But aren't you even curious what it would be like?

Iceland

To have a BOYfriend?

Me

To kiss someone who, for once in your life, makes the ice in you burn.

The display stays black for so long that I decide to start the engine and drive home after all. I probably overestimated him, and he's really not yet ready to take this tremendous leap into the unknown. Shame. Forgetting the snowflake won't be easy after the intense moments we've shared since last Friday night.

With a regretful sigh, I pull away from the curb and thread the car into traffic. Just then, my smartphone gives a tiny *pop* on the passenger seat, and I frown at it sideways. At the next red light, I grab it and read what Raffael replied. A smile cramps my cheeks.

Iceland

Maybe. A little...

That's all I wanted to hear. Instead of driving home, I take the bend around the block and head back to Brook's Mew, parking outside Raff's apartment building when a dark green Jeep vacates a spot right in front of the door as I arrive.

After I turn off the engine, I grab my pack of cigarettes and climb out of the car. Leaning against the door, I ignite a Marlboro and drag in a deep lungful of smoke. While I blow it out in a long stream, I write one last message to Raffael, making sure I'm not crossing any deadly lines again like I did when I stroked his fingers at Starbucks.

Me
Can I come up?

I've finished the cigarette by the time his answer comes in.

Iceland
Okay.

Leaving my hat behind in the car this time, I head to the front door of the building that opens with an easy push. Last time I came here with Tanja, we used the main elevator, the one that stops outside the apartments and isn't secured with personal codes. The ride to the ninth floor is short, and when the doors open, the entry to apartment 37 at the end of the hallway already stands ajar.

Okay...

I run a hand through my disheveled hair and quietly enter without knocking.

CHAPTER 10

Raffael

My gaze wanders up at the sound of someone closing the door. Sebastian. He stands at the entrance to the living room, hands in the pockets of his ripped blue jeans, hair unruly, sleeves of his black dress shirt rolled up to his elbows. His deep chestnut eyes are trained on me. Looking at them, a shower of star-spangled shivers trail through my body.

I'm still sitting in the same place where I sat a half-hour ago as we texted back and forth. They were scary messages. Exciting. And dangerous. They set all sorts of feelings inside of me free. Wrong feelings. A longing for something that I shouldn't even be thinking about.

But it's so hard not to think about forbidden kisses when this guy finds all the right words to provoke me. He makes me want to be someone I don't want to be. How is this supposed to work?

He's still standing just above the single step that leads down to the sunken living room, looking at me. As if he's waiting for an invitation. Or for... I don't know. For me to get up and lead the way upstairs to the playroom?

My tongue sticks to the roof of my mouth. I barely find my voice. My gaze briefly drops to my bent knees, my feet resting on the coffee table. But as if a part of me is afraid he might suddenly come closer—or leave again—my eyes snap back up to him. It takes an eternity for me to manage a tiny, raspy, "Hi."

He takes the step down to the same level as me. I involuntarily wince. Immediately, he stops. Then he slowly lowers to sit on the five-inch step. Forearms braced on his drawn knees, he loosely laces his fingers and keeps looking at me. I'm sure he wouldn't be so...cautious if we were already upstairs.

Slowly, I remove my feet from the table, one at a time. Rising from the couch makes my heartbeat speed up. I need to even my breaths, or I won't be able to speak with him at all tonight. I skirt the coffee table, eyes fixed on him the entire time, and cross the living room. With three feet of distance between us, I pass him at the difference in the floor level and head for the kitchen. He turns his head to watch me go.

"Want something to drink?" I ask quietly.

"No, thanks," he replies, just as calmly.

From the upper shelf in the fridge, I grab a green can of Sprite and gingerly close the door again. I should go back to the couch, but I don't make it there. In fact, I can't bring myself to walk past Sebastian again so I just stop a couple of feet behind him. It looks as if he's gazing out the window, but when he hears the fizz of my drink when I pop the tab, he turns his head again and presses his mouth against his left shoulder.

Him being here feels like the ultimate intrusion in my apartment. In my world.

He can't see more than maybe the shadow of me

on the floor. But as I drink, I keep my eyes trained on his back, his tanned neck, and the black chaos that is his hair. Standing above him helps to bring back a feeling of balance. Both inside and out.

I take two slow steps closer to Sebastian, still behind him but slightly adjacent. My legs have probably entered his field of vision now. He doesn't move. Not an inch. My heart gets a chance to settle back into a slightly faster than average beat.

I stay there for another solid minute, then I walk back to the couch. Sebastian's gaze follows me once more. This time, I take a seat a little closer to the entrance of the living room and put the can on the table, next to the scratchpad and pen that always lie there for scribbling down passwords for games and profiles.

We lock gazes again. The minutes tick by. I don't know why he hasn't said anything. Or why *I* haven't. But the longer the silence stretches between us, and the longer he sits there unmoving, letting me just look at him, the more I can relax in my apartment again. It's almost as if he's trying to give me time to adjust to being around him by remaining a still item in my world.

I reach for the Sprite again and lift it to my mouth. My eyes lowered, I ask against the lip of the can, "Wanna play some video games?"

The corners of his mouth lift slightly, and I want to smack myself for finding it attractive. I don't even know why he smiles now. Because I'm finally talking to him, or because the suggestion is up the pole?

"Sure," he says, and it sounds as if he actually means it, as if he likes the idea. "You have *Need for Speed*?"

I nod.

Then Sebastian scrunches up his face with doubt. "Are you any good at it?"

Seriously? In answer, I lift an eyebrow. "I've been playing it since I could hold a controller."

Laughing now, Sebastian rises from the step. "Well, that gives me two years more experience than you have. You don't stand a chance, Iceland."

With a small grin on my face, I put the can back on the table and fetch two controllers from the shelf beneath the glass top, holding one out to him. He comes over and takes it. "Will you jump out of the window if I sit too close?" he teases me, and I notice how his fingers brush against mine, but it doesn't seem as if that was on purpose. Regardless, it feels nice.

"Probably," I admit, glad that it sounds only thirty percent truthful, the rest a mocking reply to his banter. Sebastian refrains from planting himself right next to me, and instead slumps down on the adjacent part of the couch. That, however, puts him in the best place for playing because he's facing the huge flat-screen directly, and I have to look at it a little from the side. Damnit.

We go online, and both log in with our player accounts, then we laugh as we notice that the two of us have each rebuilt our own cars for the races. There's now a pimped-out white Honda next to a carbon-gray Corvette, waiting for the green lights to flash and the game to start.

We do a few training laps, checking out each other on the street. Sebastian is good. Definitely as good as I am. Whether he's better? I doubt it. For two rounds, I take the lead, and he's so close behind me that he can snoop up my exhaust fumes. "What's up?" I taunt him, having everything perfectly under control. "Not enough power under that hood to overtake me?"

"You bet there is, snowflake," he drawls with a grin in his voice. "I'm just enjoying the nice view of your stunning ass. I always fuck from behind."

Eyes wide, my head snaps to the side. I wreck my car against a house wall. Sebastian laughs as he takes the lead and zooms across the finish line ten seconds later.

He winks at me, his laugh reduced to a magnetic smile. While I reset a new training lap, he leans forward, reaches for my Sprite, and takes a sip. When both cars wait at the scratch line again and the countdown flashes on screen, he puts the can back in the exact same place it was and reclines on the couch to race me once more.

We both give our best, and it really is impossible to say who's the better player. It's nice to do this for once—laugh with him, sit in the same room and not panic whenever he even moves a tiny bit. I really start enjoying myself, the evening, and also the sharing of my drink. Pressing my lips to the spot on the can where his mouth was only minutes ago gives me all kinds of memory flashbacks. Of kisses and touches and him softly saying, *"I'd love to see you again..."*

After half an hour of simple training on various racetracks, I reach for the Sprite again, and Sebastian asks me, "Ready for a proper race?"

The can is light, and I shake it. Empty. Damn. "Sure." I stand from the couch and put my controller on the table. Since Sebastian's feet are stacked on the coffee table, and his legs block my way, I have to step over them to get past him. For a moment, it puts me in a very odd position. The insinuating smirk from Sebastian isn't much help as our gazes get stuck on each other. I clear my throat and move on. "Set up whichever course you like."

Electronic beeps chime out as he clicks through the menu to search for a track he wants to do, and then he enters two players. In the meantime, I head to the fridge and take two Sprite cans out. With one in each hand, I stop rigid and look at them for a second. Then one goes back into the refrigerator, and I kick the door shut.

Back in the living room, I open the Sprite, set it on the table, take my controller again, and sit down right next to Sebastian. I don't want to step over his legs again. Besides, this *is* the best place for gaming.

The slight tilt of his head in my direction doesn't escape me. His tiny smirk makes him look gorgeous. I answer with a tight-lipped grin of my own and then face the front where the game waits. "Ready?" I demand.

"Born ready." Sebastian releases the pause mode, and the countdown begins. The engines of both our cars roar, impatient to race when the big white *GO* finally flashes on the screen.

Just as the times before, it's a neck-and-neck race, except that Sebastian doesn't fool around with feeling up my ass anymore. Our cars fly down the street, taking curves at dangerous speeds, drifting and hitting the gas again. We're halfway through the circuit when Sebastian states without warning, "Winner gets a wish."

There's no time to look at him or I risk wrecking my car again from surprise, but instantly, a prickle of unease starts at the back of my neck. Not because I don't want to have a freebie if I win. I just doubt that I'll like what he dares me to do if I lose. I can't even protest, but from the sound of his voice, he wouldn't let me get out of it anyway. So, I concentrate really hard and, thirty seconds later, the Corvette shoots across the finish line. I actually completed the lap by setting my own personal record.

Except it's still thirteen-hundredths of a second behind Sebastian. "Fuck!"

He throws his arms up into the air, still clutching the controller, and cheers, "Winner!" Yeah, he's good like that, rubbing salt into wounds.

Pouting, I drop my hands into my lap and scowl at the screen that shoots fireworks for the white Honda. I've always been a sore loser. In a carefree move, Sebastian claps his hand on my thigh. "Don't be sad, snowflake. You can't win all the time." Then he grabs the Sprite and takes a sip.

I'm still sitting rigidly next to him, staring at the spot where his warm hand was a second before. My heart suddenly races as if *it* is trying to win the game.

It's so strange that his touches always ignite two very different sensations within me.

Absolute panic.

And a thrill to try it again.

"So, what's your wish?" I demand, turning a cynical grin at him. "Pizza for dinner?"

"Not quite." Laughing, he leans back and then studies me for what feels like an eternity. His lips remain in a very slight smile, but the warmth really comes from his eyes. I have no idea how he does it, but I can't look away.

He's so close, one of us would only have to move his arm a little to touch the other. And the longer we stare into each other's eyes, the more a craving to do just that grows within me.

"Fuck, Sebastian, say what you want, or I'm going to die here!"

Another moment passes. He enjoys teasing me. "Nervous?"

He can't even imagine!

"No." I work hard to find my cool again. A slow breath helps. "Because I'm not going to touch you. Or let you touch me. That's stuff for the playroom, not the rest of my apartment."

"And that's your biggest fear?" He honestly wants

to know; his tone is free of any taunting this time. "Touches?"

"At the moment? Yes." Getting up, I fetch a water bottle from the kitchen. I've had enough of the sweet stuff for tonight. "So, make a wish, and then let's play again."

He quietly waits for me on the couch, tracking my steps with his eyes. By the time we're sitting next to each other again, his mouth has curved into a tiny smirk. "All right. I want you to do something then."

While he takes the last sip from the Sprite can, my brows lift, questioning him. Holding the empty can in his lap, he drawls, "I dare you to tell someone that you entertain the idea of going on a date with me."

I laugh. "Yeah, bite me!"

"Later," he promises with an intense look of passion.

Immediately, goosebumps rise on my skin. *Everywhere.* I swallow, and he just smiles.

"Go on, then," he prompts me. "We can meet your neighbors, or just head down so you can tell some stranger on the street. Your choice."

"You can't be serious."

Except, he is.

Ugh. I suck my bottom lip between my teeth and deliberate. "Just *any*one in the world?"

"Anyone *living and breathing*. And it can't be Tanja," he defines and then sneers. "You may call your parents, if you want."

As if! But the phone call gives me an idea. "All right. Challenge accepted," I say and meet his expression with a little bit of cynicism. "Do you know how to play *Fortnite*?"

With skeptically drawn eyebrows, he nods, so I push the controller back into his hand, grab mine again, and log into the game. We quickly create a new player account for Sebastian, and then I have him meet my team. Or the part of it that is online right now, which makes two. Carol with the *Sailor Moon* profile picture, and Tom, who's using one of himself with his face hidden beneath a Yankees cap.

For those times when Felix is here, and we play some shit together, there's always a second headset on the shelf. Putting on mine, I hand the other to Sebastian, then turn on the mic and say, "Hi, guys!"

Carol cheers when she notices me log on, and

Thomas rumbles a deep "Hello," in his rolling Scottish brogue.

"I've got a friend over tonight who'd love to be a guest player on our team. Would that be okay with you?"

Sebastian activates his gaming headset and starts laughing. He obviously figured out how exactly I'm going to fulfill his dare. After both of my team members welcome him into our small group, Carol fires away, "Sebastian, can you do me a huge favor, please? Tell us what Raffael looks like!"

I don't even try to suppress a chuckle because I knew this was coming. She's been pestering me for over half a year now to give her a description of myself. There's just a picture of the Corvette against the sunset on my profile and, hands down, I enjoyed teasing her about it.

"Well, Carol, I believe you'd be smitten by Raff. He's a gorgeous Icelander," he replies and turns to me with an idiotic grin. "He looks like a real snowflake. Fragile and tall, all Nordic and blond... with a smile to die for."

Even though my brow slightly rises at his

description, I can't help but let a tiny smile slip, too. It's from the very warm feeling he creates inside of me with his words. Still holding his gaze, I speak into the mic a moment later. "By the way… I'm entertaining the idea of going out with Sebastian. And, yeah, he made me say that because I lost a race, and he tries to convince me that I'm actually interested in guys."

The chuckles from my friends drift through my headphones. I can hear Sebastian's laugh in Dolby surround sound, both inside and out.

"And are you?" Thomas asks lightly with a nonjudgmental tone that I appreciate.

"What, gay?"

"Yeah."

"I'm not exactly sure about that," I say in a sarcastic way that clearly means: *No*.

"Doesn't matter," Sebastian chimes in, his focus on the game now that we've started. His tone is rye and sweet as he says, "I'll help him figure it out."

Carol giggles into her mic. I'd rather not know what kinds of pictures he just painted in her mind with that comment.

We head out together on a zombie hunt and blow up one of their camps. But more of the brain-eating suckers ambush us and suddenly, we're all cornered in the woods near the fort. Damn, we need Leo and George. Doesn't look like we're getting out of this alive.

"Iceland, we have a problem," Sebastian deadpans and makes me laugh.

But then his phone rings and, after pulling it out to quickly check the caller ID, he brushes down his gaming headset. "Sorry, people, I've gotta take this." He puts the call on loudspeaker between us to keep his hands free for playing. "Hi, Claudia, what's up?"

There's a picture on the display of a woman in her early thirties with black hair and the same eyes as his. She holds a little girl in her arms. Both smile; the toddler behind a sucker in her mouth.

"Hey, Bash. You have a minute? Michelle has been speaking about you all day. I doubt I'll get her to sleep if you don't say goodnight to her."

"Sure. Turn it up." He waits a second, concentrating on the screen, still trying to get us out of the zombie trouble, then he continues, "Hey, baby doll. How you doing?"

Instantly, the surprised and joyful, "*Maah*" around a sucker drifts from the speaker. It turns the corners of my lips up.

"You don't wanna go to sleep?"

"Bash...come?"

"Not tonight, baby doll, but soon. Promise." While he speaks with evident love to the little girl, he accepts that we've just lost the battle on screen. The idiot lets his avatar drop to his knees and scoots closer to mine until his face is in my avatar's crotch. Carol and Tom laugh their heads off, which only I can hear because Sebastian doesn't have his headset on.

Unmoved by my elbow jab against his biceps, he just grins and continues talking to the girl. "You gonna sing with me again when I come?"

"Winko, winko, eebie shar..." the unintelligible words come from the girl, but the melody of her voice makes it clear that she's actually singing *Twinkle, Twinkle* to Sebastian.

"No, not that song." He laughs. "You know which one."

I don't know where to concentrate: on the game or on Sebastian, who's having the loveliest conversation with someone I believe is his niece. The one he told me he wanted to catch a unicorn for. Since we're already dead, I decide to focus on Sebastian.

"We'll sing our cool song together when I come to visit you, okay?"

"Vizzi now?" she asks, the longing in those two words apparent. He must be a great uncle to her if she loves him so.

"No, not now. I have to work this weekend, baby doll. But soon."

"Bash...where?" Her voice is getting fainter, and next, the laughter of her mother chimes out.

"Oh, no. She's looking for you at the door now," Claudia whines, obviously smitten.

"Naaaawww..." Sebastian scrunches up his face with a torn smile. "Get her back on the phone. I didn't get my kiss yet!"

"Seriously, Raffael," Carol suddenly murmurs in my ear. "If you haven't made up your mind about the gay thing yet, you should absolutely give it a try with this guy. He's ad*ooo*rable."

Yeah, I can see where she's coming from. My heart is actually melting a little, too. I'm just glad Sebastian didn't hear what she said; he surely wouldn't let me live it down.

There's a rustle on the line while Claudia apparently chases the toddler and then tells her to throw a kiss to her Uncle Bash. A very wet-sounding smack rings out that almost has me sighing with Carol. Sebastian throws her one back, then Claudia speaks again. "Don't make her wait too long. She misses you terribly."

"I miss her, too. Both of you." Sebastian picks up the phone and clicks off the speaker, holding the device to his ear. "I'll call you tomorrow from work as soon as I know when I have a few days off... Hug the baby... Yeah, bye." He lowers the phone, presses the red disconnect button, and shoves it back into his pocket. Then he puts the headset back on and apologizes for the interruption.

Carol doesn't hesitate even one second to chime in, "Bash! Can I have a baby with you?"

Tom and I crack up, while Sebastian only purrs

salaciously into the mic. They flirt shamelessly for about a minute, but then I interrupt with a grin. "We better stop this here before the game turns into a dating hotline."

"*Jealous?*" Sebastian mouths at me with a teasing fire in his eyes.

I only mouth back the word, "*Nooo.*" Then we both say goodbye to the others, and I turn off the PS4.

Only now do I notice how time has actually flown by. It's past nine o'clock; Sebastian has been here for almost three hours. The sun has set behind the roofs of the city and, without any lights burning in the apartment, it's quite dim in the space.

We put the headsets and controllers back on the shelf under the glass top of the coffee table, and I consider getting up and switching on the reading lamp on the other side of the couch. It's just that I find it extremely hard to move when Sebastian captures me with his gaze in a way that makes my skin burn. All silent and intense.

After what feels like an endless moment, he quietly asks me, "Can I make a wish again?"

"Another dare?" I rasp.

"Sort of." He tilts his head just a little bit. "But this time, you can say no. I won't wind you up with it."

I swallow. "What do you want?"

And he says... "Touch me."

CHAPTER 11

Raffael

"Where?"

The word is a barely audible whisper from my lips. Sebastian and I sit in the dim evening light of my living room, and suddenly, I'm all too aware of his scent of musk and sun-warmed skin. Only a couple of feet away from me, his long legs stretch across the gap between the couch and the coffee table, and while his left hand rests on his stomach, the other arm lies on the cushion next to his hip.

He wants me to touch him. And for once, there's a deep need inside of me to stretch my limits and just reach out.

"Anywhere you want," he replies. His voice slings a loop of soft caresses around me in the semi-darkness. "It's all right if you want to just touch my hair."

Automatically, my gaze moves to his forehead where a few strands of chaos nearly brush his eyebrows. A strange curiosity grabs me. How might it feel? Soft? Thick? If I lean in now, will it smell of warm summer days, too? My heart riots in my chest because I'm too scared to find out.

I pull my feet onto the seat and twist a little more in his direction. His chestnut eyes hold the last light of the day, and his full lips rest in an easy, barely-there smile. A five o'clock shadow accentuates the lines of his face, the stubble as dark as his hair, making him look wicked.

I never let my beard grow. It comes in very sparse and is so light, it would make me look as if down feathers grew on my skin. I always shave clean as soon as the first stubble is detectible, like every three or four days.

My fingers itch to stroke Sebastian's black whiskers, but his face is too dangerous a ground to start with for my first touch. The top two buttons of his black dress shirt are open and reveal the extensions of the Maori tattoos that run from his right wrist upward to hug his shoulder and chest. His left forearm holds none. There's only this simple, gorgeous, black leather bracelet where most people wear their watch. Not him, though. His watch is fastened around his right wrist, looking like a seam to the tattoos that stop just short of his hand.

Concentrating on my breaths, I reach out and then let my fingers hover right above the many black inked lines on his forearm. They lie between us like a dangerous snake of temptation that I'm now allowed to explore. For a final, short check, my gaze returns to his face. His focus is on my hand, but one blink later, his eyes find mine, and I swallow. For one quick moment, the corners of his mouth lift into an encouraging smile before they return to their relaxed position.

Very slowly, I lower my hand and begin tracing one of the dark Maori tattoos. It runs in a zigzag pattern across his skin. I shove my finger along the line to the middle of his inner forearm, feeling the warmth of his flesh.

My heart races.

Where the tattoo ends, a new one that looks like a queue of overlapping diamonds starts. Following their outlines gives me time to warily wander upward to where the pushed-back sleeve of his shirt begins. It's like a barrier that stops me from exploring any further. I bite the inside of my cheek.

As if sensing that I need a lane to follow, Sebastian cautiously reaches for his sleeve and shoves it up over his biceps. My throat dries out a little. There's a double track of square spirals there that I peruse, one by one. His arm is strong, displaying the power that bleeds from every inch of him. It takes an eternity to get higher until the black fabric stops me again. From here, it's only a small jump to the dark ink on his collarbone, peeking from under his shirt.

"Why do you follow those lines?" he asks in a low, husky voice.

A moment passes as I consider. "I find them calming."

"Most people find them irritating. Too much chaos in one place."

Focusing on his eyes again, I keep my fingers motionless. "No. There's a beautiful order to this chaos." My breaths are shallow but slow.

His calm gaze says that I can go on, and there's a promise there, too. One that says he won't make me tell anyone about touching him, and that I might enjoy it a lot more than I want to admit.

Reluctantly, I lift my hand and set the tip of my index finger down on the outermost curve of the tattoos on his chest. There's some ink to trace within the space of the top two open buttons. While I run my fingers over the entire area around the collar of his shirt, the hush in the room presses against my ears. Jesus Christ! What am I doing?

Sebastian watches me the entire time. I feel his stare on my face as I concentrate on the Maori tattoos. I swear he can tell what I'm going to do before even *I* know it because he places his hand over mine the moment I think about pulling away from him.

A prickle of shock runs through me, and I hold my breath. His palm is a little callused, but his grasp is gentle. Damnit, my throat dries out. I let him move my fingers down and then feel how he undoes the third button of his shirt with both of our hands, our fingers almost laced now. After another button loosens, he leaves my hand on the tattoo that only covers part of his chest, ending near the curve of his pec. He opens the rest of the buttons, and the thin black fabric of his shirt slides down either side of his torso, revealing a hard, flat stomach.

His smooth skin is flawless there—and inkless. My fingers stop at the verge of leaving the tattoos. I cannot go on. I just can't.

When Sebastian suddenly leans forward, I jerk my hand away. Stretching his arm, he grabs the blue pen that lies on my notebook on the table and then reclines back into his former half-lying position. With a determined look down at his body, he begins drawing a zigzag line on his skin, right beneath his sternum.

Instantly, my forehead creases into a frown. "What are you doing?"

Sebastian smirks, but he doesn't look at me. "Drawing you a street map to follow."

What the fuck?

I throw my hands over my face, laughing into my palms as I glance at the ceiling through my spread fingers. Then I drop them and rise, but Sebastian grabs my wrist fast and hauls me back down to the couch. I snap my head to him and sit rigidly as he keeps my hand in his. "Don't run away," he pleads softly, tilting his head, his eyebrows slightly drawn.

"I wasn't. I just wanted to..." *Get up and dash to the kitchen where I can sit in the fridge and cool off. Fast.* Okay, perhaps that sounds a little like escaping, but I really don't know what I'm doing here. Fuck, Sebastian is a guy. *A. Man!* And a damn gorgeous one, too. When I think about touching him again, strange waves of adrenaline rush through my body so quickly, it feels as if I won't be able to cope much longer and will just have to knock myself unconscious by banging my head against the wall.

"Sometimes, when you look like that," Sebastian begins and gives me a little smile, "I'd love to know what you're thinking about."

I blink free of my caging thoughts and let his gaze carry me for a moment. "Fridge. Walls. Unconsciousness..." I murmur and then sigh, closing my eyes.

His chuckle is something I could get used to in quiet moments like this. It sounds comforting. And nice.

The leather couch creaks when Sebastian sits up. Suddenly, his hand molds itself to the side of my neck and cheek. My eyelids open a little, my gaze fixing on the hole in his blue jeans.

He leans forward, close to my ear, and his mouth brushes my skin in a husky whisper. "Enough touching for tonight." He pushes himself up from the couch and quickly arches his eyebrows once as he shrugs on his shirt. His lips compress when he finds me staring at him. "Take care, Raff." Then he turns and heads to the door, closing it quietly behind him.

I stare at the silver doorknob for a moment before a groan finally escapes me. Squeezing my eyes shut, I tip sideways against the backrest of the couch. Bloody hell!

This is *so* spiraling out of control. Men in my apartment. Guys seducing me. Well, one... But he's got a smile that totally unhinges me. Every damn time. And there's nothing I can do to make everything right again. To put myself—and most of all, my feelings—back to square one. Where is this all heading? To me thinking about kissing a guy? To me *longing* for it?

Well, congrats. We're already there.

Grunting with frustration, I run my hands through my hair and then head upstairs to take a shower. A long one. Ice-cold. My body freezes, but it doesn't help to get rid of the fucking thoughts circling in my brain. Jesus Christ, I'm so doomed.

Back in the kitchen thirty minutes later, I make a sandwich and plant myself in front of the TV. Distraction. That's it. All I need is a distraction. I could play some *Fortnite*. But then Carol would only dwell on the thing with Sebastian, and that won't be much help either. Instead, I grab the remote and flip through the channels. There's some stuff on the news about the upcoming Gay Pride Parade again, and I'm really not up for *that* now. I find a thriller that I've already seen three or four times, but it's good enough to keep me occupied.

Until my phone beeps on the coffee table.

For minutes on end, I stare at the blue light

flashing in slow intervals. The entire time, it feels as if my heart is making a trampoline out of my tongue. What if it's a text from Sebastian?

But, if I'm completely honest, that's not what makes me so nervous all of a sudden. It's the chance that it might *not* be him. And then...? Would I be disappointed? Pressing my lips together, I close my eyes and sigh, because...

I think I would be.

After a few deep breaths, I finally lean forward to fetch the phone. The smile that comes next makes me bite my lip with the wish to destroy myself. This is so fucking crazy. And still...in a dangerous, scary way, it's nice.

I read Sebastian's message a couple of times and then let my thumbs jerk across the keys, typing a reply.

Sebastian

You still alive, or did you jump from the roof after I left?

Me

Still alive.

Sebastian

But the thought appeared...

I lick my lips and laugh.

Me

*Oh yeah, it did. Actually, it keeps crossing my mind
back and forth.*

Sebastian

:-)

Me

You think this is funny?

Sebastian

No. I find it awfully sexy.

Sinking deeper into the couch, I mute the TV and
angle my legs, my feet on the edge of the coffee table,

holding the phone against my thighs.

Me

That you can make me jump from roofs?

Sebastian

That I can make you break your own rules. And get past your limits.

Me

What do you think my limits are?

Shit. What do *I* think they are?

Sebastian

Right now? I believe a kiss would be quite hard for you.

Okay, comes pretty close. I frown at the display. How the heck does he know me so well? He seems to read me like a car magazine—with too many sexually explicit pictures in it. I inhale deeply and suck my bottom lip between my teeth.

Me

That's not in the cards.

Sebastian

Yet. ^^ But that's okay. We'll go slow.

Me

Slow? You had me watch you fuck my friend.

God, so many images flood me at that memory, I have to squeeze my eyes shut and groan...because there's a bulge building in my jeans. Holding my phone a little higher, I glare at it. *Go away! I don't need you right now!* Maybe I should go take another shower. In a barrel of ice cubes.

Sebastian

I'd have much preferred you beneath me instead of her.

I don't like that vision. But I like that he thinks about it. *Argh!* Please, somebody kill me! Now!

Me

You think this is even possible?

Sebastian

Anything is possible as long as you don't go all Iceland on me again.

Me

This is really tough, you know. Everything about it. I hardly know what I'm doing anymore.

Sebastian

Are your hands shaking?

Odd question. I scowl at my hands. Then I laugh and type away, starting with the smiley that covers its eyes in shame.

Me

A little bit...

Sebastian

Raff?

Me

Bash?

Sebastian

Would you go out with me?

Fuck, no!

My eyes snap wide like popcorn. Expelling a gasp, I rake my fingers through my hair.

He must be on his second bottle of whiskey to even think there's any chance.

Or...*gosh*!

Me

Um...

Sebastian

Come on, don't be scared. It's not like a romantic date. Just going somewhere, doing things together.

I must be taking too long with my answer, because he breaks the balance of the chat and writes another text.

185

Sebastian

But we can go to the movies, too, and watch Cars *if you like. :P*

Yeah, he can shove the sticky-out-tongue-smiley he added right up his ass. However, it makes me think, and soon, I draw in a breath through my clenched teeth as I write.

Me

Just going anywhere? Like…a club party?

Sebastian

Sounds like a good place to start.

Me

The summer term at uni ended. There's a little celebration at The Knockout in Soho tomorrow.

There'll be hundreds of students there, primarily people I don't even know. I'll go with Tanja and Felix. They certainly won't mind if we hang out with Sebastian for a while, too.

Sebastian

Cool club. You want to meet there?

What I really want is to set my life back two weeks and be who I was for twenty-three fucking years. But...

Me

Yes

And then I write another message really fast to beat him to the next text when I already see the wave of dots saying he's typing a reply.

Me

But this is not us going on a date, holding hands, or doing some such shit together. Understand? We meet there, we talk, we hang out. That's it.

Sebastian

LOL. Cool off, snowflake. I'm not going to kiss you. In public...

Jesus Christ. I roll my eyes and moan.

Me

Night, Bash.

Sebastian

Night, Iceland

P.S. Your fingers felt amazing on my skin today.

I let my head fall back, close my eyes, and feel a searing heat soar up my neck.

CHAPTER 12

Raffael

The day flies by, and no matter how hard I try to grasp onto each hour, the evening comes much too fast. After a shower, I pick a white polo shirt from the closet where Rosa put the freshly laundered clothes this afternoon and pull it on. The hem sits loosely over my bleached blue jeans. Next, I head into the bathroom, run my hands through the chaos on my head and, bracing my hands on the marble basin, look into my eyes in the mirror.

Damn. I'm not ready for this.

Straightening, I lace my fingers behind my neck, let my head fall back, and blink at the ceiling.

Sure, I told Sebastian this wasn't a freaking date or anything, just us meeting somewhere in a club. But I'm not stupid. I know what his intentions are. He may not have had a chance to screw me in the playroom at the beginning of this week, but that doesn't mean he hasn't dreamt about it.

And I... I actually don't know what I'm dreaming about anymore. I only know that, suddenly, there's a damn lot of Maori tattoos in them.

After switching off the light in the bathroom, I run downstairs and slip into my dark blue Adidas, grab the car keys, and head out. Tanja and I wanted to be at the club by ten. It's already a quarter past. She's going to kill me. Or laugh because I'm *never* late.

I drive the few blocks to her apartment, park at the curb, and leave the engine running while I shoot her a message: *Come down, pumpkin. You can hitch a ride with Cinderella's hottie.*

Two minutes later, the car door opens, and Tanja throws herself into the passenger seat. The girl looks fabulous in tight jeans and an even tighter, simple gray tee. She grins broadly in my direction. "Hi,

Cinderella." Her black ponytail slides over one shoulder as she provocatively strokes the dashboard and lowers her voice to a loving caress. "Hi, hottie."

"Ha. Ha." While she buckles in, I grab the inside of her thigh and pinch her until she squeaks and swats my arm away. Moving my hand to the gear shift again, I check my side mirror and then ease the Corvette into traffic. The Knockout isn't very far, only a few minutes from here.

"You're late," Tanja utters, but the few words hold a questioning edge and speak volumes.

"Yeah." I don't want to say more about it. It's mortifying.

But, of course, she doesn't let it go, no matter how hard I concentrate on the tail-lights of the double-decker bus in front of us. "You never are."

"Well, today I was."

"Why?"

"Jesus, Tanja! Can we drop this subject, please?" I avoid looking at her, even though her curious gaze bulldozes a hole into my skull. Besides, she knows the answer. She didn't let me get off the phone for over an hour this morning when she heard that

Sebastian might be coming to our end-of-the-year celebration. Not until she squeezed every last little detail out of me regarding my time with him on the couch.

"Don't be so negative," she scolds me and looks front again, for about two and a half seconds. Then her gaze jerks back to me, and a bright smile edges her voice. "It's cute that you took so long to get styled to meet Sebastian. And he'll appreciate it, too. You look *hawt*! I told you a million times, you should wear polo shirts more often."

"I didn't take so long getting pretty for him," I growl, throwing her an evil sideways glance that usually promises some discipline later. "I was looking for ways to escape."

"Yeah. That's what you say. But I bet your heart is doing double-flips when you think about him."

Pressing my mouth shut, I give her a quick look and then glance front again because she hit the nail on the head.

Fuck! My life is one ugly mess these days.

Felix doesn't know about our extra guest yet. I wonder if I can convince him that it was total coincidence when Sebastian shows up. Probably not.

When I slowly drive up the street that houses the club and scan the place for a parking spot, Tanja suddenly touches my arm. It almost makes me jump. I don't know why, perhaps because she never does that when I'm driving. Or maybe because I'm just way too edgy tonight.

Her intense look promises that whatever she plans to say next doesn't require an answer. So, I'm quiet as she speaks. "I'm glad it's finally out, Raff. This special thing inside you. At least now, I know it's never been about me." She shrugs, and her smile is honest and warm. "You just don't fancy girls like you want to, is all."

Clenching my teeth, I keep looking for a place to park and then reverse the car into a spot around the corner. I turn off the engine, and Tanja slips out of the buckle harness, ready to climb out. I do, too, but then I grip the steering wheel and rest my cheek on my hands for a second. "Tanja?"

She turns around, her fingers still on the door handle. They slip away, and her hands fall into her lap then she meets my gaze. I know how lost I must look. I heave a deep sigh and briefly close my eyes. "How can it be that I didn't notice for over twenty years that I'm attracted to boys?"

She takes a long time to consider her words, her glance repeatedly wandering out the window behind me. "Perhaps because you didn't give yourself room for it with all the control you keep over yourself." Then she firmly strokes my head twice, flattening my hair before it springs into place again. Her smile turns from soft to teasing. "And perhaps you kept control so much because it allowed you to ignore the truth."

Her words sink in and sit with a gravity that makes my stomach dip. My gaze moves past her to the corner of the street where the club's name flashes in bright blue and pink neon. Sebastian may already be here. A long, deep breath escapes me, drying out my throat. "I don't want to go in there," I whisper.

Tanja plays with my hair a little more and then caresses my neck. "I know..." She clasps her handbag and grins. "But I also know something else."

"What?"

"That you're actually *dying* to get in there and see

him again."

Slowly, the right corner of my mouth hikes up. Yeah, I guess I am.

Happy with my silent answer, Tanja gets out and waits for me on the sidewalk. We round the corner to the club entrance, and while I hold the door open for her, she spins around in front of me, skips a couple of steps back, and cheers, "Okay, let's get drunk! Let's dance! Let's party!"

My smile is restrained because, other than Tanja, I have no idea what awaits me tonight.

Happy, she pulls me through the short hallway and into the club, escaping people on the way. The music gets ever louder, yet it's still a level of volume that allows one to talk to others without shouting—if they stand really close. The entire place is tinted in ultraviolet light that occasionally changes from blue to pink. There's a dance floor in the center, bursting with people bumping and grinding under the strobe light. Tanja loves to shake her stuff and will most likely join them in half an hour. She'll pester me to come with her like she always does. I'm not a good dancer—or eager to learn. But enough friends from uni are here tonight, and they will be happy to take my place. Maybe Tanja will get Felix to dance with her for once, although I doubt it.

We see him at the bar ahead. He's having a drink with Nikki, Elliot, and three people I don't know. Aiming straight for the group, I force myself not to let my gaze skim the place. No need to run into Sebastian within the first two minutes.

Tanja reaches around Felix from behind and covers his eyes. Totally unnecessary for him to guess when she asks who it is; not when he knows the feel of her hands, the smell of her perfume, and the gentle sound of her voice. He turns around, taking her wrists and pulling her in for a hug and a kiss on the cheek. "Hey, you two. What took you so long?" He lets her go and smacks his hand into mine for a greeting. We briefly press our shoulders against each other with our arms between and clap the other on the back.

"I couldn't find my keys," Tanja saves me from the embarrassment of telling my friend that I was just plain nervous and stalling. "What are you drinking?" She grabs his glass with some bluish liquor from the bar, sniffs it, and then takes a sip. Likely to change the subject.

Felix lets her have his drink and orders new ones. It's a rum and Coke this time. The second drink, a plain Coke with a lemon slice is for me. He knows my drinking habits—I have none.

"Cheers," he says as we all clink glasses. "To three months of doing nothing for you two, and all the more work in the shop for me over the summer."

I grin and take a sip. He loves his work and always complains about vacations being too long.

"By the way," he continues and sets his glass on the bar, still keeping his fingers around it, and his arm on the counter. "Sebastian is here, too. I met him in the back a few minutes ago."

The instant rise of my heartbeat is annoying as hell. As is Felix's grin. I don't know what my face just gave away, but he's good enough at reading me. He's had years and years to learn. God, I hate being trapped inside this body at the moment. Bloody traitor.

The club is big but not huge. If you're looking for someone, you only have to take a walk around and you'll probably spot them in under five minutes. I don't. Instead, I grip my glass harder and focus on my friends, trying to follow their conversation—for all of twenty seconds. Then my eyes start flicking to the side as if they have a mind of their own.

I'm cool. I'm relaxed. I don't give a shit, I tell myself. Until my gaze gets stuck on a guy some twenty feet away, who's wearing his black Nike cap backward on his head. My heart does the first real somersault of the night, jumping right into my throat.

Sebastian is talking to a woman in high heels and a red mini dress. Two guys in jeans and some band t-shirts flank the woman, one standing so close that he can undoubtedly smell the brand of her toothpaste while she smiles at Sebastian. The other keeps a little distance from her, but that's probably because he seems more interested in what the guys are saying than in her.

Sebastian hasn't noticed me yet, which is good because I really need a moment to gather myself. Loyal to his dress code, he came here in a dark gray t-shirt with a black button-down shirt on top, left open. One hand is in the pocket of his jeans, the color a little darker than what he usually wears, and without any holes for once. He holds a bottle of beer in the other hand. From beneath his short sleeves, I can see the tattoos snaking down his right arm. They add an extra layer of heat to my already prickling skin and remind me of the intense hours in my apartment last night.

"Go and talk to him," Tanja hisses next to me, taking the Coke out of my hand.

Instantly, I make sure that none of our other friends heard that, but they're occupied with Felix. We're safe. So, I shoot her a sharp scowl. "I can't."

"Why not?"

"Because—" Yeah. That's it. My reason. Feeling totally out of my depth, I turn back in Sebastian's direction. Straight away, I want to bang my head on the bar because he looks really good tonight—and heck, I can't believe that I just noticed that.

Lifting the bottle to his lips while the shorter of the two guys speaks, he blinks slowly. When his eyes come open again with the next flash of the strobe light, they're set straight on me.

I freeze.

I gulp.

I can't look away.

So much for: *he hasn't noticed me yet.* He knows exactly where I am, probably watched me from the moment I walked into the place.

He takes a slow sip of his beer, then his cheeks blow up with the gulp before he swallows and lowers the bottle. His gaze is still nailed on me. Holy fuck! My body is stiff like granite.

Only when he moves his attention back to his friends, do I find the strength to spin around. Tanja is my anchor. My buoy in the storm. The one I focus on with terrified eyes to keep me from panicking and leaving the club. Cold sweat prickles on the nape of my neck.

"Goodness, Raff! You're such a baby!" She laughs.

"Shut up," I growl. "This isn't funny. I feel like..." Shit, I don't even have a word for what I feel.

"Like a teenager crushing on someone for the first time?" she teases me.

Seems about right. "I wouldn't know."

"Because you've never fallen for anyone before."

I narrow my eyes at her and add a layer of reproach to my tone. "Could you please stop this? Or at least don't speak so loud." Point made, I quickly look at the others standing around us, but she keeps giggling and pats my cheek.

"You're so cute. I really didn't think I'd ever see you so excited, sweetie."

"You know what? I don't feel like partying anymore." I drink the rest of my Coke and put the glass back on the bar. "I'm going home."

"To escape Sebastian?"

"Yes."

Her perfectly plucked brows tip together. "Then you better hurry up."

"Why?"

A body brushes lightly against the right side of my back. Goosebumps zing all over my skin. "Hi, Tanja." His words come in a friendly voice next to my ear. From the sound of it, there's a half-smile on Sebastian's lips, one that Tanja mirrors as her eyes move a little upward to meet his gaze behind my shoulder.

"Hey there! How great that you came," she replies

and then swipes her blue drink from the counter. "I'll leave you two alone so you can—"

Instantly, I grab her wrist and pull her right back to where she was for the past five minutes, cutting off her words with a sinister warning. "Don't you *dare*."

Her smile is for Sebastian, the sheepish look for me. "Or maybe I'll just stay..."

Beneath the odor of dry fog and liquors that are so apparent in the club, a light fragrance of musky shower gel crawls up my nose. Damn, it's so creepy to feel his stare on the side of my face when I'm unable to move even an inch in any direction, let alone look at him.

With my forearm on the bar, my fingers clench around the empty glass. At least I have something to hold on to, even if it's something breakable where I should really reduce my force.

Sebastian places his beer on the counter, right next to me. His fingers touch my elbow almost discreetly as they wrap around the bottle. His arm is stretched out behind me this way, and his entire body remains flush to the side of mine. "Well, summer break now, huh?" he asks Tanja when I still haven't said a word to him ten seconds later. "Going anywhere for vacation?"

While she tells him that she's probably going to see her grandparents in Wales for a week or two, all I can concentrate on is the man behind me who seems to sweat dominance from every pore. His warm breaths stroke my neck as his chest rises steadily against my back. Even the music seems to have softened so that I can hear the sound of every inhale.

The heaving of my chest is twice as fast as at the beginning, but my breaths gradually ease, matching his rhythm. Only my heart is still all over the place. And my tongue sticks to the roof of my mouth.

"Yo, Rhyse," Felix interrupts Tanja as he suddenly appears next to her with both his hands on Elliot's shoulders, steering the Japanese guy over to us and in front of Sebastian. "This is Elliot Kimito. He's part of the scene, organizing races and shit."

Sebastian steps away from me, getting all business-like as he shakes hands with the slender programming student.

"Elliot had this great idea to arrange a special

match," Felix continues. His gaze briefly switches to me. I just frown.

"The crowd loved how you performed last time out in Enfield," Elliot explains, his eyes wide with enthusiasm. "We think that a race between the two of you would cause an impact like a bomb. No risk for you. People would bet money on the outcome. What do you say?"

Sebastian stands more beside than behind me now, and this time when he turns his head to me, I look him straight in the eyes. My blood begins to sizzle, but I refuse to let any emotion show.

Eventually, he shrugs, keeping his nonchalance. "Sure, why not?" Then he takes a sip of his beer. Turning my head to Elliot, I give a terse nod.

"Fantastic!" Elliot punches Sebastian's number into his phone and adds him to the exclusive racing group we run on WhatsApp. "We'll set it for a Friday night. Probably in two or three weeks, but we'll let you know soon enough. You good with that?"

We both agree and watch him return to the others standing nearby. Felix's obvious intention is to follow him, but Tanja puts a spoke in his wheel and forces him to escort her to the dance floor instead. The little witch is so fast, there's no chance for me to object this time.

Suddenly, I'm all alone with Sebastian in the thick of a group of strangers.

Panic surges through me once more, and I pivot to brace both forearms on the bar, spinning the empty glass between my fingers. With so many people in the club, it takes a while until the bartenders get caught up with all the drink orders. It gives me some time to decide whether I'll have another Coke or a Sprite instead.

"You going to talk to me at some point tonight?"

Angling my head, I look at Sebastian next to me and immediately see his arched eyebrow. Before he can say more, I cast a quick glance over my shoulder to where my other friends are. No one's watching us, but even if they were, it probably just looks as if we're talking about the upcoming race.

"What you wanna talk about?" I mumble, but it feels a lot better to scowl into my empty glass instead of meeting his gaze again.

"No idea, Raffael, really. But a simple *hi* would

have been nice for a start."

I close my eyes for a tortured moment before I'm brave enough to turn toward him. "Hi."

"See? That wasn't so hard, was it?" He takes a sip from the beer and then puts the bottle down, his expression turning a little grim. "And nobody thinks we're going to fuck right here on the bar because of it."

I stare at the glass in my hands. "Don't they?"

"No, Raff. Shit, *no!*" Gripping the bottle with both hands on the bar, he takes a small step back and drops his forehead on his arms. "Men speak with each other everywhere, every day. It doesn't automatically mean they're in a relationship."

The last word makes my gut churn. "I don't want to be in a relationship." *With you.*

"I'm not asking you to," he growls between his forearms. Then he straightens and expels a breath. "All I want right now is to hang out with you."

Hanging out yesterday meant me telling people that I might be into boys and then later moving my hands all over Sebastian's body. How am I supposed to cope? I wipe my thumbs up and down the misty glass and focus on the lemon slice drowning in the melting ice inside. "I don't think that I'm the right person, even just for that."

"Can you look me in the eyes when you say that?" he demands, and not very happily.

I swallow. It takes me a while to lift my head. His gaze on me is so intense, my throat tightens, and my voice turns raspy. "This is all going too fast for me. I don't want to be like this."

"Like what?" he snarls. "Bisexual?"

Jesus Christ, he shouldn't use that word with me. I squeeze my eyes shut. "It's not what...I am." When we came here, I thought I could deal with this. With him. With myself. With the unfathomable attraction. But the truth is, I can't.

Sebastian waits for a long moment. And only when the silence gets unbearable and I look up, does he say in a harried tone, "You honestly want to tell me that guys don't interest you more than girls?" He shoves one hand into his jeans' pocket and almost crushes the bottle with the other. "That you didn't enjoy yesterday evening with me? Didn't feel anything while we sat on your couch and you kept sneaking side glances at me?" His expression gets even darker as he leans in closer. His voice drops a deadly notch. "While you touched me."

Of course, I felt something. In fact, I've never felt so aware of myself before.

But they were all the wrong feelings. Nothing good can come of this. It seemed so much easier outside in the car when I spoke to Tanja about it. Sitting here now, confronted by the man who gives me sleepless nights, is more than I can bear at the moment.

"I'm not gay. Or bisexual. Or whatever," I murmur, once again escaping his gaze. "I can't give you what you're looking for, so it's probably best if you just drop the idea and find someone other than me to hang out with."

A moment ticks away. "Find someone else..." he repeats, and I can't decide whether his tone is disbelieving or if it's just him weighing the words. Probably a bit of both.

I give a small nod and hate the tight feeling in my throat. What the fuck is happening with me? If he doesn't leave right now and turn things back to how they were before I met him, I'm going to crack.

Sebastian sighs and, from the corner of my eye, I can see him pucker his lips, clearly deliberating. Eventually, he smacks his palm flat on the bar as if he's come to a decision. "You know what? You're right," he states flatly. "Obviously, you're not ready for this. Why should I waste any more time with you?"

Whoa. Lance straight to my heart. My head snaps up without me wanting it to.

"The night is still young, and I hate sleeping alone on the weekends." His cold sneer adds a burning tip to the lance in my chest. "Take care, Raff."

And then he walks away.

Depressed, hurt, and confused as fuck, I let my head hang, ignoring the young woman on the other side of the bar who finally has time to take my order. When she goes to the next patron and then mixes a cocktail, someone else takes the seat to my left.

"You look miserable," Tanja says, placing her hand on my arm. "The conversation didn't go so well then, hmm?"

"Actually, it went fantastic," I grumble. "He finally

understands that I don't want anything from him."

"You told him that?"

I nod.

"Why did you lie to him?"

This is bullshit. I push away from the bar. "Be right back." Not waiting another second, I stride off through the crowd and take the narrow hallway to the restrooms. While there's an endless queue in front of the ladies', the space in front of the gents' is deserted. One brave girl with pink hair and a black hoodie comes out when I slip inside. She gives me a quick smile, which I force myself to return as I hold the door open for her.

Once alone in the restroom, I brace my hands on the edge of the simple, white washbasin and glare at the reflection of myself. I'm not gay. Definitely not. Gay people look different. I look the same as I have the past few days, weeks, and months. I'm not into boys. I fuck girls in my playroom. I've kissed Tanja a million times.

Bloody hell, I'm just. Not. *Gay!*

After splashing some water onto my face and drying myself with a couple of paper towels from the dispenser, I head back to the club and slide onto a barstool next to Tanja. She's talking to Felix and two girls I've seen her hanging out with a lot at the university this year, but I don't know their names. A few people from my architecture courses flitter around in the club as well, but I don't have the nerve to meet them and celebrate right now. I'd much rather celebrate alone. Sebastian is gone. I'm straight again. Victory? Who cares?

When the bartender with a black club shirt asks me again what I want to drink, I place my car keys on the counter and order a bottle of Eristoff Ice.

"Are you all right?" Tanja demands softly after she's detached herself from her friends and now stands closer to me. Her concerned gaze takes in the vodka, the keys, and then my eyes.

Instead of answering, I lift the bottle's neck to my lips and take a large swig. Not bad. Let's see how many of these buddies I can down before the club closes.

"Raffael, I'm worried about you. Maybe we should call it a night and go home," she says beside me while my gaze is nailed on the shelves stocked with liquors behind the bar.

"Or grab a burger somewhere, what do you think?" Felix suggests, obviously no longer interested in Tanja's two friends.

A burger sounds nice. More vodka sounds nicer. "You two can do whatever you want." I cast them a stern glance. "I'm fine. Stop worrying."

"You're drinking," Tanja points out, dead serious.

"So what?" I shrug. "You two drink all the time. And I can take a cab to Mayfair. I won't wreck my car tonight."

"That's not what we're worried about, man," Felix says. "You ain't gonna—" And then he breaks off because two guys come to lean on the bar on my other side, one of them wearing a black Nike cap backward on his head.

Filled with utter shock for no reason, I turn, my eyes way too wide. Sebastian stands with his back to me, close enough that I can feel the heat of his body. He doesn't say a single word, but over his shoulder, I can see the infatuated gleam in his younger companion's eyes. I know him. The guy with the brown curls and a gray sweatshirt is Noah Scott. He's twenty-two, and he studies architecture with me.

Sebastian orders a beer and a Red Bull for them, then they clink drinks and laugh as they continue a very flirtatious conversation, which they clearly started a few minutes ago.

"I think we should leave now," Tanja's grave voice drifts to me over the pounding bass. But I only shake my head.

Even though I doubt that Sebastian knows that Noah and I are classmates, he obviously brought him over here for a reason. They could have found any other place to flirt with each other in this goddamn club. But he chose the spot right next to me to demonstrate something.

Well then... Go ahead.

With my elbow propped on the bar, and my gaze stoically leveled on the shelves ahead again, I let some cold liquid seep into my mouth, swish it around once, and then swallow. I don't need to watch them. It's enough that I can hear them and feel Sebastian's body much too close to mine.

Felix's and Tanja's solicitous silence from my other side is almost as annoying as the fucking lovebirds to my right.

"Hey, Raff!" Noah blurts all of a sudden, leaning half around Sebastian on the bar. "I wasn't sure if you were coming tonight."

"Noah," I murmur nonchalantly against the mouth of the bottle in greeting. I like him. He's cool. But right now, I'd rather he wouldn't talk to me. Neither of them.

My Fairy Godmother doesn't favor the desperate. My wish gets denied.

"So...you two know each other?" Sebastian's intrigued voice holds a secret sneer as he turns around to me. "That's great. You take any courses together at uni?" In my peripheral vision, he lays an arm around Noah's neck and pulls him closer. My chest constricts a little.

"Math, 3D modeling, and drawing," Noah replies with a snicker. I'd guess he has a handful of drinks on me.

"Is that so?" Sebastian drawls, and I make the mistake of turning a tiny bit in their direction, ignoring Tanja's hand on my arm. Sebastian pulls Noah really close and brushes his nose across his cheek. "Then you're going to be an architect, too?" he groans salaciously into Noah's ear.

I bite the inside of my cheek until I taste blood. Why the fuck can't they find a quiet booth somewhere else?

"Raffael..." Tanja whispers—almost pleads.

I briefly close my eyes and growl low enough for only her to hear, "Leave me alone." She takes her hand away, exchanging a worried glance with Felix, but he knows better and just shakes his head. After a frustrated-as-hell sigh, she grabs a fistful of peanuts from one of the many bowls on the bar and throws them into her mouth.

Sebastian's mouth, on the other side of me, still hangs on Noah's ear, doing all kinds of things—licks and nibbles. Noah has shut his eyes and, leaning with his back against the bar, simply enjoys the treatment he gets from the guy I feel so strangely drawn to.

My throat is dry like the grasslands in Australia. I take another sip of the vodka. It helps shit.

As close as they are, I can see every move they make, even if I don't want to. But just like it is with accidents, they're horrible to watch, yet you still can't look away.

When Sebastian starts kissing a trail from Noah's ear toward the corner of his mouth, everything inside me convulses. I wish so desperately that the feeling would go away. That I could just throw the bottle against the wall and leave.

Or that he would stop.

But he doesn't.

Noah lifts his hands to Sebastian's chest, slowing him down just a bit as he murmurs, "You think this is the right place to go there?"

"We can leave if you want," Sebastian answers. "My car is parked down the block."

I think I'm going to be sick.

Noah's voice turns needy. "You have enough room in that car?"

"It's a nice car. You'll like it," Sebastian drawls, pushing his hand beneath Noah's sweatshirt.

And there's just one fucking word pushing into my mind.

CHAPTER 13

Sebastian

I want Raff. More than I've ever wanted anyone or anything before.

I've never had to deal with inexperienced boys. Everyone I've met so far has been well aware of his sexuality and celebrated it. There was never a need to be careful or to go slow. But with Raffael, it's all different.

What he did last night—the shy touching on the couch—was like the sweetest thing I've ever seen or experienced. And it made my heart pound in a way that it hasn't in a long time. I was ready to take every cautious step necessary to ease him into this whole new world. He could have taken all the time he needed to figure out the monumental change happening inside him. I figured I could wait.

But if he shuts the doors without even giving us a chance, my patience comes to an end. He wants me to fuck off and find someone else? Fine. I can do that. Let's see how he likes it.

Bringing Noah to the bar to fool around with him was intentional. That I picked one of Raffael's classmates for it was not. Either way, the guy seems nice, and he's easy work. I don't need to sweet-talk him for an eternity. If I want to fuck tonight, he'll be game.

A bottle of vodka stands in front of Raff, and it catches my attention. I don't know many things about him yet, but I know that he doesn't usually drink alcohol. The keys to his car lie next to it on the bar. So he wants to get drunk? Well, maybe it'll do him some good for once.

Tanja's pleading look from behind Raffael is hard to ignore. What does she expect from me? Her friend lives in a world full of crappy rules that say he mustn't fall for a man. Accepted. I'm not going to touch Raff ever again. Before we part for good, however, the snowflake needs to see that two men can actually have some fun together and not instantly combust in the flames of hell. No one around us is watching. And those who are, are mostly smitten girls who clearly find this quite attractive.

Raffael needs to learn that times have changed since the Stone Age. And people's attitudes have, too. I may not be the one doing all these sweet things to and with him for the first time. But one day, somebody will. And for his sake, I really hope he can let himself be free when that happens and just enjoy it.

A muscle starts ticking in Raffael's jaw when I loop my arm around Noah's neck. *Yeah, it hurts, doesn't it?* Wasn't so great to be sent to hell by him before either.

Noah is going to be a frustration fuck tonight— but certainly a good one. He's not even my type, he was just the easiest to find in a few minutes. If I wasn't getting off with him, he'd have fallen into the next guy's arms and found some fun there. I appreciate noncommittal sex.

But I would've loved to share a drink with Raffael tonight so much more.

Grinding my teeth, I fight to ignore his tense composure on the stool next to us and concentrate on seducing Noah instead. The sooner we get out of here, the better. Although I might have to stop breathing too deeply when I nibble his ear because the dude uses a brand of aftershave that makes my stomach tighten with revulsion. And he put a lot of it on.

I brush my lips in a line toward his mouth, ready for the first real taste of him. He's drinking Red Bull. Not something I fancy, and it will undoubtedly spoil the flavor of the kiss. Why do I want to push a fucking Sprite down his throat right now? Ugh.

My lips hover half an inch above the corner of his mouth. It only takes one small move from me. My eyes flash to the side, finding Raffael's torn gaze focused on us. His face is pale like snow while he clasps the Eristoff bottle with all the force needed to turn it into a diamond.

Not my problem. Fuck him. He made it clear he doesn't want anything from me. Doesn't even want to give us a chance.

No more kisses. No more touching. No more video games at his place.

His throat twitches as he swallows. There's a silent plea in his look. For me to stop? Why should I?

I close my eyes, expelling a breath I didn't even know I was holding, and bring my lips down on Noah's mouth.

"Titanium…" The sudden, hoarse croak wrenches from Raffael's throat.

And I freeze.

To be continued…

ANNA KATMORE
Broken
DAWN

BROKEN DAWN

The rules in Raff's playroom allow me to get into his pants. But breaking Titanium is so much harder.

After Raffael stuns me speechless in the club, it's time to change the rules of our game a bit. He gets to decide when he's ready to kiss me. But everything else will be my decision from now on.

Sebastian is the most dangerous dare I've ever had to deal with.

His touch springs the chains from a passion I didn't know was bound inside of me. Nothing has ever felt so forbidden...and yet so good at the same time.
My world comes unhinged.
And I don't know how to put it to rights again. Or if I even want to...

More books by Anna Katmore

ON THIN ICE
Counting Fireflies
Splintered North

*

Seventeen Butterflies

GROVER BEACH PLAYERS
Play With Me
Ryan Hunter
T Is For...
Dating Trouble
The Trouble with Dating Sue

FALL FOR ME
The Impossible Bet
Taming Chloe Summers

CRUSHED HEARTS

Unfair Love

Broken Dawn

Awaking Trust

ADVENTURES IN NEVERLAND

Neverland

Pan's Revenge

THE TRUE CHRONICLES OF FAIRYLAND

A Prince for Little Red Riding Hood

A Wolf in her Way

*

Eloyn

You were my Fairytale

My Secret Vampire

Three Shades of Sinful

About the author

"I'm writing stories because I can't breathe without."

At six years old, Anna Katmore told everyone she wanted to be an author after she discovered her mother's typewriter on a rainy afternoon. She could just see herself typing away on that magical thing for the rest of her life.

In 2012, she finished her first young adult romance "Play With Me" which was the beginning of her true writing career, with many books to follow.

Today, she lives in an enchanted world of her own, where she combines storytelling with teaching, and she never tires of bringing a little bit of magic into the lives of her beloved readers, too.

Anna's favorite quote and something she lives by:
If your dreams don't scare you, they aren't big enough.

For more information, please visit:
www.annakatmore.com

www.ingramcontent.com/pod-product-compliance
Lightning Source LLC
Chambersburg PA
CBHW021154160726

47994CB00001B/202